The Weaver

The Weaver

Dr Sheetal Nair

NU VOICE
PRESS

First published by NU VOICE PRESS 2025
An imprint of Hubhawks Pvt. Ltd
www.nuvoicepress.com

This is a work of fiction. Space and time have been rearranged to suit the convenience of the book. Except for public figures, hotels, and institution names, any resemblance to persons living or dead or the real events are purely coincidental. The opinions expressed in the book are those of the characters, and should not be confused with that of the Author.

ISBN: 9788199425484
Typeset by Pooja Sharma
Printed at Thomson Press (India) Ltd
Published by Nu Voice Press

*For **Siddhansh**,*
my bravest teacher, my smallest philosopher,
and the reason I learnt that
we don't raise children—they raise the parts of us
that never grew safely.
And for every silent struggler who has outgrown pain
but not yet found peace.
You were never alone.
You were simply never spoken to in your language.

Author's Note

Why This Story, Why Now?

They say stories no longer matter.
That attention spans are shrinking.
That people want speed, not depth.
Clicks, not questions.
Content, not meaning.

They say that books like this—slow, thoughtful, unhurried—will only be read by the few.

And to them, I say: *good.*

Because *The Weaver* is not written for the many.

It is written for the *ready.*

For those who are tired of shallow noise. For those who seek not more information, but transformation. For those who, quietly, even secretly, want to find a way back to something *true.*

We live in a time where *the loudest voice wins*, even if it has nothing to say.

A time where rage trends faster than reflection. Where we scroll endlessly, yet rarely arrive anywhere.

This book is my rebellion against that.

It's not fast. It's not flashy.
It doesn't promise to change the world overnight.

But it might change how you *listen to it.*

In these pages, you will meet Sid—a desert herder who is offered a thread and a riddle.

His journey isn't grand. It's *slow.*

He doesn't seek power or fame.

He seeks understanding. And in doing so, he begins to *weave something that just might hold a broken world together.*

This book asks you to slow down.
To read differently. To remember how.

It will not shout for your attention.
But if you lean in, just a little, it will reward you with something deeper than distraction.
It will remind you that peace isn't a dream.
It is a practice. A stitch. A shared labour.

You are not outside this story.
You are in it.
You *are* it.

And maybe, just maybe, when you turn the last page, you will no longer ask what the world owes you—but what thread you are willing to carry.

Welcome to the loom.

Dr Sheetal Nair

Prologue

The Thread Before the First Knot

Long before a story is told, it is felt:
Like a breeze before the monsoon.
Like a hush before the loom begins to speak.
Like a truth that has waited for the right listener.

This is not a tale of kings or warriors.
It is not about conquest, nor survival.
It is a story of slowness.
Of silence.
Of stitching together what was once torn.

The world you are about to enter may seem distant—a desert village, a lone boy named Sid, a whisper from the wind. But if you listen closely, you'll find that it is not distant at all.

You know this world. You live in it.
It is the world where people talk but rarely connect.
Where wells run dry not just of water, but of patience.
Where peace is a stranger, and noise is always on time.

Sid's journey is not one of distance, but of return to something we have all misplaced.

He will meet weavers, mystics, dancers, and monks.
He will learn what cannot be taught in classrooms or headlines.
He will gather not treasures, but **threads**—*of practice, of presence, of peace.*

And when he returns, his hands will not be full, but ready.

This book does not ask for your agreement.
It asks for your attention.

The loom is waiting. The first thread is yours to hold.

Step in.

Contents

I

Chapter One – The Desert Whisper

By late afternoon the dunes had forgotten their edges and melted into one another like old memories. Sid guided his camels toward the thorny silhouette of a *khejri* tree, the only splash of green on an ocean of ochre. The air quivered. Heat rose like a prayer that had lost its words.

His parents had named him "Siddhansh", but he preferred being called Sid, so the name stuck with him.

He had learned to read the desert the way other boys learned to read books. A shinier ripple meant the wind had changed. A crescent of darker sand meant a beetle had passed. A lone footprint that didn't belong to man or camel meant the desert was making room for a story. He was nineteen years old, and if you asked him, he would say that he wanted nothing—except a wind that finally blew him somewhere new.

The herd folded its legs with grateful sighs. Sid loosened their nose-ropes and tied them in a circle so they would not wander, then sat beneath the khejri. The tree provided thin shade, but it was shade nonetheless, and the desert taught you to receive small mercies as if they were miracles.

From his pouch he took out a round *bajra* roti, yesterday's, hard as a promise kept too long, and softened it with water. He tore it in half and saved the bigger half for the evening. "We bargain with life the way we bargain in the bazaar," his mother used to say, tapping his head. "Always keep a little something for later." She had died when the monsoon clouds forgot to come.

He looked toward the west, where the sun slanted low. Somewhere beyond that horizon was Ahmedabad, people said, where gold threads changed plain cloth into wedding songs. Somewhere beyond the next horizon was Ajmer, where men spun like tops, and swore they had touched God. Farther still was the river that bowed to a mountain, and the city with ghats that glowed like fireflies trapped in stone. Sid had never been to these places. Still, he carried them in his pocket like smooth stones.

The wind changed. It came from the north now, cool against the skin. With it arrived a dot that swelled into a man, then a man and a stick, then a man, a stick, and a bundle on his back. The camels smelled him before Sid did and lifted their heads. Strangers were rare, but not miracles. The desert was full of people who had lost their way or were trying to.

"Peace to your animals," the stranger called, his voice cracked like a dried riverbed. "And to the one who keeps them."

"Peace as far as the sand allows," Sid said, standing up.

The man reached the shade and smiled without showing teeth. He was older than the old, the way dunes are older than years, with eyes that held too much of the sky in them. His kurta was the colour of dust and had the dignity of a garment that had been washed in many wells. The bundle on his back was tied with a red cloth the colour of wedding vermilion. A brass ring as thin as a halo circled his staff.

"May I sit?" he asked.

"Shade belongs to whoever arrives first," Sid said. "But I reached a little earlier, so I'll share." It was a joke his father would have liked. His father had left a year after his mother, not in death but into the dry mouth of the city, where men chased work like chaff chased the wind. He had promised to send money. Promises liked to travel; money rarely did.

The stranger sat and leaned the staff against the tree. He drank the water Sid offered, then closed his eyes as if the liquid had turned his throat into a temple. "You are kind."

"I am thirsty when others drink," Sid said. He tried to sound wise. It came out as simple.

"What do you herd?" the stranger asked, eyes still closed.

"Camels."

"And what herds you?"

Sid blinked. "The sun," he said, after a moment. "And what it does to the sand. And the prices men pay at the animal fair."

The stranger opened one eye and squinted as if measuring the boy with the string of his gaze. "Ah. The small tyrants." He took a sliver of jaggery from his pocket and broke it in two. He kept the smaller half and offered Sid the larger. A man who gave away more than he kept had not always been poor.

They chewed in a companionable silence, listening to the soft belly-music of the camels. When the sun bent lower, the stranger cleared his throat.

"Do you know why the desert is a good place to hear?" he asked.

"Because there's nothing to listen to," Sid said, grinning.

"Because there's nothing to drown the truth," the man corrected, but he was smiling too. "At night it grows quiet enough for even stubborn words to return."

The light thinned to honey. A pair of chinkara leapt like brushstrokes across the fading yellow. The heat lost its teeth. The stranger untied his bundle and took out a small clay cup shaped like the palm of a begging hand. He placed it between them.

"I am a fakir," he said. "Not a very good one. I eat when I am fed and sleep when I find a tree. Sometimes I forget God while looking for God. But the wind remembers me. Today it told me to walk until I met a boy with eyes like unlit lamps." He tapped the cup. "This is for what the wind wants to pour."

Sid felt something in his stomach make room. He did not believe in prophecy the way desert men believed in water. But he believed in stories and how they sometimes needed a listener to become true.

"What does the wind want to pour?" he asked.

The fakir lifted the cup and tilted it toward his ear, as if listening for a liquid that you could hear. "A thread," he said, after a while. "A thread only you can weave."

Sid snorted. "I can mend a saddle, nothing more."

"Threads mend more than leather," the fakir said gently. "Listen: your village has forgotten rain. Not because the clouds lost the road, but because hearts did. Peace is a shy animal. When people shout, it stops visiting the well."

"Peace?" Sid echoed, tasting the word like a date he wasn't sure was ripe.

"*Shanti*," the man said, and the sound seemed to cool the air. "You will find its thread and teach your people to weave with it. The thread runs from the desert to the river that bows to the mountain, to a city where fire dances on water, to a tree that remembers a prince, and finally to a woman who spins flowers into warmth. When you return, your hands will know what your heart has been trying to say."

It was either a beautiful lie or a beautiful truth. Sometimes they were the same thing, under a sky like this.

"And what will I be paid for this weaving?" Sid asked, because boys who fed families learned to ask.

The fakir's eyes were soft. "You will be paid in a village that sleeps without locking its doors," he said. "In a well that does not go dry in men's throats. In a name that parents will give to their sons because it tastes of shade."

Sid looked away. There were calluses on his hands shaped like the ropes he pulled. He had always thought his work was to keep animals alive. The fakir's words felt like someone had untied a different rope and placed it in his palm.

"Men have walked to rivers before," he said. "They came back with fever."

"Then don't bring the river back," the fakir said. "Bring the thread." He reached into his bundle and took out a scrap of rough cloth, the kind you might use to wrap onions. On it, in thin charcoal, a couplet had been scrawled, shy of rhyme but certain of direction:

Where the river bows to the mountain's knee, seek the hand that spins stillness from a traveling tree.

Sid frowned. "Riddles are for the bored and the rich."

"Riddles are for the patient," the fakir replied. "And peace is a slow answer." He pressed the cloth into Sid's hand. The boy could feel the faint ridges of the letters, the way thoughts leave footprints.

"How do you know it is me?" he asked. "There are other boys with eyes ... like lamps that haven't been lit."

The fakir chuckled. "The wind spoke your name. And besides, you've been walking in your head for years. Your feet are only catching up."

Sid opened his mouth, then closed it. He had never left the district. And yet at night he found himself counting distances the way devout men counted beads. The bazaar's hum, the chanting at a shrine, the long bell of a river-boat—he knew those sounds without knowing them.

"How far?" he asked.

"The first step is the farthest," the fakir said. "After that, you are already on the road."

They watched the sun tuck itself behind the dunes. Evening's first star pricked the sky. The camels shifted and settled; the desert cleared its throat and grew quiet. Sid made a small fire of dry twigs and baked the saved half roti over it. He offered a share. The fakir ate slowly, as if each bite were a lesson he was trying to learn well.

"Do you have a family?" Sid asked, because sometimes questions are another way of feeding.

"Once," the fakir said. "Then the road asked to be married. She is a jealous wife."

Sid smiled. "She gives you no house."

"She gives me many roofs," the fakir said, turning his palm upward to the stars. "And I owe no landlord."

A jackal laughed somewhere, sharp and brief, the way men laugh when they are afraid. Sid felt the night grow thinner, as if it had been stretched on a loom and he could see the world's warp and weft.

"If I go," he said, "who will tend the camels?"

"Those whose work it is to stay will stay," the fakir said. "Those whose work it is to go will learn that leaving is also a kind of tending."

"You speak like a man who has never left a mother behind."

"I speak like a man who left and found his mother had been traveling with him," the fakir said softly. "In the way he accepted water. In the way he feared thunder."

The fire settled into a red eye. Sid folded the cloth and slipped it into his pouch. The weight was more than fabric; it was a direction. He thought of his father's last letter, the one that said, *Work is a river that forgets its sailors. If I am late, forgive the current.* He thought of his mother's bangles, thin circles that clinked like laughter. He thought of the well that now showed its bottom like a tired tongue.

"Say the couplet again," he said.

The fakir obliged, and the words seemed to learn their shape in Sid's mouth.

"Where the river bows ..." he began.

"... to the mountain's knee," the fakir finished.

Sid nodded. The Brahmaputra, he had heard, bent before the hills like a respectful son. The Ganga bowed before the Himalaya, priests said, the way prayer bows before silence. Rivers had manners; men were still learning.

"What is a traveling tree?" Sid asked.

The fakir smiled into his beard. "Some trees move when no one is watching."

"Now you are teasing me."

"Then watch more," the fakir said. "You will see many things that don't believe in witnesses."

They bedded down without more talk. The fakir wrapped himself in a shawl as thin as patience and slept like a coin at the bottom of a still bowl. Sid watched him for a while, then turned to the sky. The Milky Way spilled its quiet wealth. A falling star cut the dark cloth and disappeared, needle to thread.

He closed his eyes and found himself standing in a street he had never seen: lamps floating down a river like a city answering the night, bells calling men to the edge of themselves. Then a tree with a trunk the colour of old gold and leaves that did not move even when the wind pushed them. A woman with hair whiter than cotton wool, her hands moving so gently that threads became birds.

When he woke, the fire was a memory and the east was the colour of first thoughts. The camels complained, as camels do, about everything and nothing. Sid sat up and stretched and felt, for the first time since childhood, the delicious ache of a day that had already chosen him.

The fakir was sitting cross-legged, holding his cup from the night before. He turned it over in his palm and then, with a small smile, placed it into Sid's hands.

"Keep it," he said. "To remind you that you can carry emptiness without being empty."

Sid weighed the cup. It was light and cool and somehow exact.

"If I don't go," he said, "will the wind be angry?"

"The wind does not get angry," the fakir said. "It simply stops visiting."

Sid looked at his animals. He looked at the tree. He looked at the horizon that had been practicing its beckoning for years. Then he did what boys do when they love something—he tied it well, so it would not be hurt by his leaving.

He lashed the water-skins, counted the ropes, checked the hooves. He laid a hand on the khejri's bark and thanked it for being a roof. He turned to the fakir.

"If the thread is real," he said, "I will find it. If it is not ..."

"If it is not, you will bring back a way of listening that your village has misplaced," the fakir said, standing with the help of his staff. "Either way, you will not return the same."

Sid nodded. Until that moment, he had not known that he was waiting for permission to become himself.

He took the first step.

The sand accepted his foot without a comment. The second step was easier, as the fakir had promised. The third felt like a promise he had made to someone he could not yet name. By the time the tree's shade had loosened its hold and the voices of his camels had thinned behind him, Sid was on the road.

He did not look back. The desert, like pride, does not like to be watched when it is being left.

The fakir watched until the boy became a dot, then a stitch, then a thought returning to its giver. He raised his staff in a salute no one saw, then turned in the opposite direction. The wind, pleased with its delivery, wandered off to find another errand.

By noon the dunes had remembered their edges. Sid walked with the sun like an old adversary with whom he had made a truce. The cloth with the couplet warmed against his heart. The cup clicked gently against his pouch. The horizon kept moving and he kept following, as if the two were learning each other's patience.

When the day cooled and the first evening birds drew invisible calligraphy on the sky, Sid spoke aloud, to see if his voice still knew him.

"Where the river bows to the mountain's knee," he said, tasting the words. "The hand that spins stillness from a traveling tree."

The desert gave him no answer. But it did not refuse to listen.

That night, beneath a different tree and the same stars, Sid dreamed of water that did not run out when men remembered how to speak softly. He woke with his mouth wet and did not know if it was from the dream or the wind.

He smiled. He walked. The road widened to receive him.

When the world grows quiet enough, even a whisper can become a map.

DSN

Chapter Two – The Merchant of Ahmedabad

From Khejri he walked until his path joined the old road out of Ajmer, the same road that wound its way toward Ahmedabad like a patchwork quilt sewn from centuries. Dust and stone made up its seams, stitched together by the relentless tread of traders, wandering monks, camel caravans, and dreamers whose hopes had risen and fallen under the same burning sun.

Sid followed it for days. Sometimes he walked alone, the silence stretching between him and the horizon until it felt like another companion. At other times, strangers fell into a step beside him—a farmer on his way to sell *ghee* in a distant village, a young man with nothing but a flute and an easy smile, an old woman carrying pots of pickles she swore could heal any heartache. They would share fires at night, the flames painting their faces in gold and shadow.

The desert here had a different rhythm from the one he had known. The dunes were gone, replaced by flat, baked earth that held the dull gleam of old copper. The air shimmered, heavy and slow, as if weighed down by the sun itself. Thorn trees stood scattered across the land like stubborn sentinels, their roots sunk deep in defiance. By the fifth day, the wind carried a new scent—faint at first, then growing stronger: jaggery, fresh dye, and something else. A heat-born metallic tang, like the scent of coins warmed in the palm.

The horizon sharpened. What had been a mirage resolved into towers, domes, and rooftops pressed tightly together as if huddling for protection. The city gates rose ahead, massive and still, like the calm blink of an animal that had seen countless travellers pass through. It neither welcomed nor repelled; it simply existed, confident in its permanence.

Ahmedabad.

The moment Sid crossed the gates, the air itself seemed to rearrange. The streets became narrow threads, pulled taut through the loom of the city, weaving one quarter into another. Life here was movement and pattern—hawkers calling from carts stacked with vegetables; women's voices bargaining in rhythmic cadences; the metallic ring of a blacksmith's hammer echoing against copper pots. The scent of fried *pakoras* mingled with the sharper tang of indigo dye. Women in mirrored *ghagras* seemed to carry pockets of sunlight in their steps, while children, hair wild from the wind, ran with kites tucked under their arms.

There was colour everywhere. Reds like the bleeding edge of a desert sunset, blues as deep as the promise of monsoon clouds, and gold—glimmering not just in jewellery or temple domes, but in delicate threads being drawn out and twisted by the hands of artisans.

The zari bazaar lay tucked away in a corner of the old city. It was smaller than Sid had imagined from the tales he had heard, yet it pulsed with the quiet confidence of a place that knew its worth. Here, gold was not locked away in chests; it was coaxed into filaments so fine they could slip through the eye of a needle. Stalls overflowed with saris that shimmered as though holding captive a piece of the sun. Men examined shawls by lifting them towards the light, as though waiting for the cloth to speak. Women haggled, not because they doubted the value, but because the ritual was part of the purchase.

The air was warm with the faintly sweet scent of burnt silk—the singeing of stray fibres to smooth the weave. Sid paused in front of a shop no larger than a camel's pen, its shelves stacked high with folded cloth that seemed to hum softly in the dim light.

Inside, a plump man in a spotless white kurta bent over a length of fabric. His spectacles were pushed so far up his forehead they looked like a second brow. Without looking up, he spoke.

"You have the look of a man who cannot decide whether to enter or keep dreaming at the threshold."

Sid stepped inside, the floor cool under his tired feet. "I'm looking for work."

The man's eyes, sharp but not unkind, flicked up to meet his. "Work? Can you weave?"

"No."

"Stitch?"

Sid shook his head.

The man folded the fabric with deliberate care. "Then why should I keep you?"

Sid held his gaze. "Because I can learn faster than you can tell me I can't."

For a moment, the man's face was unreadable. Then, a chuckle rose from him—warm and unexpected, like ghee sizzling in a hot pan.

"My name is Viren. You will carry spools, fetch tea, and sweep the floor. And you will watch. Watching is cheaper than learning, but it lasts longer."

Life in Viren's shop unfolded like a careful weave. Mornings began with sweeping the fine layer of dust that the market left behind each night. Sid learned to fetch tea from the stall across the lane, balancing clay cups so not a drop touched the silk. He carried spools of gold thread from the storage chest to the worktable, each one delicate as a sigh.

The loom fascinated him. Viren's hands seemed to speak a language Sid could not yet understand—adjusting tension, feeding the thread, guiding the shuttle. The gold thread was temperamental. Too sharp a pull and it frayed. Leave it untended and it curled. Treat it carelessly and it knotted into a stubborn snarl.

"Gold," Viren said one afternoon, his eyes never leaving the loom, "is like dignity. Once broken, it is hard to restore."

The shop became a crossroads of human stories. A bride-to-be came with her mother, her fingers trembling as they traced sari borders. "I want to look like a goddess," she whispered. An old man brought in a shawl his late wife had worn, asking for a tear to be mended. "She laughed in this shawl," he said, as though joy were a fragile confession.

One day, a merchant from Kutch arrived with cloth so coarse Sid winced at its touch. Viren examined it as though it were a fine heirloom. "Sometimes," he told Sid later, "it is the plain weave that holds the strongest memory. Not all stories need gold to endure."

Over weeks, Sid's hands learned the loom's secrets. He found the balance between coaxing and commanding, between speed and patience. His back no longer ached from sweeping; his grip steadied when carrying the delicate spools. He began to hear the market's daily breath—the rush of morning, the long exhale after noon, the gentle stirrings as evening approached.

One evening, after they had closed the shutters, Viren poured two glasses of water.

"You've been here long enough to know that gold thread is not about luxury," he said. "It's about light. People come here because they want their cloth to catch light—and in catching it, hold a memory still for a little longer."

Sid thought of the fakir's words about the thread of shanti. Could peace be like gold thread? Thin. Stubborn. Precious because it refused to be rushed.

Days passed into weeks. The rhythm of work and the murmur of the market became part of him. Yet Sid knew he would leave soon.

On the morning he made his decision, Viren was bent over the loom, gold dancing in the light. Without looking up, he said, "You are going."

"Yes."

Viren tied off the thread and met his gaze. "Journeys are like weaving. Pull too hard and the thread breaks. Pull too little and the pattern never forms. Walk at the pace of your own stitch."

From a shelf, Viren took a small spool of gold thread and placed it in Sid's hand. "Not for selling. For remembering. When the road tests your patience, touch this. It will remind you that the finest things take time, and the hand must be gentle."

Sid tucked it beside the cloth with the couplet. Two small tokens, yet they felt heavier than his pack.

As he stepped into the bazaar, the city moved around him like a vast loom—voices the warp, colours the weft, and smells the dye that bound them together. And for the first time, Sid felt himself to be not just a traveller, but a thread in a pattern still unfolding.

Patience is the loom on which peace is woven.

Peace and purpose are woven slowly, one patient stitch at a time.

DS

Chapter Three – The Sufi of Ajmer

The road from Ahmedabad to Ajmer was a ribbon of dust that wound between fields of mustard and patches of scrub, then climbed steadily into the Aravalli hills. The days grew cooler, the nights sharper, and Sid felt the weight of his gold thread spool and the fakir's cloth shift in his pouch as though they were restless too.

He passed through villages where women pounded grain in wooden mortars, their bangles keeping time with the rhythm. Children ran beside him, asking where he was from and whether he had sweets to share. He gave them the dates he had bought with his last coins. In the evenings, he slept near roadside shrines, the flicker of oil lamps keeping the dark from feeling too large.

On the third day, the air began to carry a strange blend of fragrances—rosewater, sandalwood, and something richer, like the memory of a feast. Alongside it came music, faint at first, then swelling: the slow throb of a drum, the cascade of a harmonium, voices layered in yearning.

Ajmer.

The city unfolded like a prayer bead string, each turn of the lane leading to another bead of noise, colour, and devotion. The streets were thick with pilgrims from every corner of the country—men in skullcaps, women in bright dupattas, children clutching their parents' hands.

Hawkers called out their wares: garlands of marigold, *chadars* embroidered with gold, incense sticks wrapped in paper cones.

Sid followed the crowd until the walls around him gleamed white in the sun. Ahead, an archway opened into the courtyard of the dargah of Khwaja Moinuddin Chishti, its marble glowing like cooled milk.

Inside, the air changed. The noise softened into a hum, and the scent of roses thickened until it clung to his skin. Pilgrims moved slowly, as if the stones beneath their feet asked for respect. At the far end, a group of men in long white robes turned in slow circles, their arms outstretched, their eyes closed. They spun to the beat of a single drum, each rotation steady, each movement as precise as the turning of the earth itself.

Sid watched, transfixed. Their robes flared like petals, their bare feet kissed the marble with each step, and their faces ... their faces were serene in a way he had never seen in the desert or the bazaar.

An elderly man in a green turban noticed his gaze. "First time seeing the whirling?" he asked, his voice warm.

"Yes," Sid admitted. "What are they doing?"

"They are dervishes," the man said, eyes following the circle. "They turn until the self grows dizzy and lets go. In that emptiness, only the Beloved remains."

"Why turn?" Sid asked. "Why not sit still?"

The man's smile deepened. "Because the world itself turns. The earth spins, the stars spin, the galaxies spin. The soul remembers its place in the dance by moving."

A younger dervish, perhaps only a few years older than Sid, broke from the circle and approached him. His face was flushed, his breath even. "Join us," he said simply.

Sid hesitated. He had two left feet, and the idea of spinning in public made his stomach flutter. But the fakir's words came back—*Peace is a slow answer.* Perhaps this was part of the answer.

He stepped into the circle. The dervish showed him how to plant one foot, pivot on the other, and keep his eyes soft. At first, Sid's turns were clumsy. The marble swam beneath him, and the courtyard blurred. But slowly, the drumbeat stopped being an instruction and became a pulse in his own chest.

Something shifted. The edges of his thoughts softened. He no longer worried about his balance or how foolish he looked. The air moved around him like water, and he let it. He felt the gold thread in his pouch grow warm, as though it too were spinning in place.

When the music stopped, the dervishes slowed one by one, their robes settling like quiet waves. Sid stood still, swaying slightly, his breath deep.

The young dervish smiled. "What did you see?"

"Nothing," Sid said. Then, after a pause, "And everything."

The dervish nodded, as though this answer was always the right one. "Remember—keep turning, even when your feet are still. The road ahead will feel lighter."

Before leaving the courtyard, Sid approached the tomb of the saint. It was draped in an ocean of embroidered chadars, the air thick with prayers. He took the spool of gold thread from his pouch and laid it briefly on the cloth, letting it absorb the blessings of the place. Then he wrapped it again, feeling its weight had changed. It felt neither heavier or lighter, but deeper.

As he stepped back into the streets of Ajmer, the drumbeat followed him, not as sound but as rhythm—a reminder that even in stillness, the world is moving, and he with it.

Surrender is not giving up; it is giving in to the dance of the world.

DSN

Chapter Four — Varanasi Dawn

The river had been following Sid for days, though he had not yet seen her.

At first, she was only a rumour carried by traders on the road—a cool wind at night, the taste of silt in the air, a faint hiss beneath the cries of market sellers.

Then she began to speak in small ways: the smell of wet earth before dawn, the sight of a boat pulled high on a muddy bank, the cry of water birds he had never heard in the desert.

When he finally saw her, it was as if the earth had pulled back a curtain.

The Ganga.

She appeared between fields of sugarcane and groves of tamarind, her waters wide and slow, holding the morning light like a secret.

As Sid drew closer, he felt a strange mix of excitement and humility, as if approaching someone who already knew all his questions and was in no hurry to answer them.

Varanasi was already awake when he reached her ghats. Bells from a hundred temples swung in unison, their sound layered over the deep, rolling chant of priests. The air was thick with the smoke of incense, the sharpness of marigolds, and the faint iron tang of the river.

The ghats—broad stone steps leading into the water—were alive. Women in saris of every imaginable colour carried brass pots to fill with river water for puja. Old men sat cross-legged, murmuring mantras as they rolled prayer beads. Children leapt shrieking into the shallows, splashing one another as though holiness could be caught like fish.

Near the base of one ghat, a group of men gathered around a body wrapped in white, marigold garlands laid across it. Sid watched as they placed it gently on a pyre, the flames taking hold slowly, then with determination. The smoke rose straight into the pale morning sky. A few steps away, life continued without pause—a woman wringing out her hair, a chai seller clanging his brass cups.

A boatman caught Sid's gaze from the water. His hair was white as river foam, and his skin weathered into deep lines that looked carved by the current itself. "Boat ride?" he called.

"I have little money," Sid replied.

The boatman's smile was missing a few teeth but none of its warmth. "Give what you can. The river takes many currencies."

Sid stepped into the narrow wooden boat, feeling it rock under his weight. The boatman pushed off with his oar, and soon the ghats began to slip past like pages in a book being turned slowly.

They drifted in silence for a while, the only sound the dip and pull of the oar. Sid watched the city from this new vantage: stone steps stained by centuries of water, temples leaning slightly toward the river as though listening to her, pilgrims bending low to touch her surface before bringing their fingers to their foreheads.

"You see that ghat there?" the boatman asked, nodding toward one where the flames of another pyre reached skyward. "That's Manikarnika. The fire there has been burning for longer than anyone remembers—centuries without pause. Ashes go to the river, and the river carries them away. Birth, death, joy, grief—it all passes through her hands."

"Doesn't it tire her?" Sid asked.

The boatman chuckled. "Tiredness is for those who try to hold on to what passes. The river knows better. She lets go the moment something arrives. That's why she never runs out of space."

They passed a group of boys in a smaller boat, drumming on overturned buckets, their laughter keeping time with the beat. A sadhu sat cross-legged in another boat, eyes closed, palms upturned, his face painted in white ash. Two herons stood perfectly still in the shallows, waiting for the right ripple.

Sid thought of the fakir's couplet—*Where the river bows to the mountain's knee*. He had not yet seen that bow, but he felt the truth of it in this place: bending was not weakness, but a form of grace.

The boatman rested his oars and let the current take them. "You've come a long way," he said, studying Sid.

"I can see it in your shoulders—they're carrying more than they were made for. But the river will teach you something."

"What?" Sid asked.

"That the water you try to cup in your hands always escapes. But if you let it rest in your palm without clenching, it stays longer."

Sid smiled faintly. "Is that how peace works?"

The old man's eyes crinkled. "Peace is a river. Hold it too tightly, and it slips away. Let it flow through you, and it makes you part of itself."

When they returned to the ghat, Sid reached into his pouch and pressed a coin into the boatman's palm. The man didn't look at it. "When you find what you're looking for," he said, "don't knot it too tight. Even a sacred thread must breathe."

Sid climbed the steps slowly, his feet feeling heavier with the weight of the lesson. The gold spool and the cloth in his pouch seemed warmer now, as if they had absorbed a little of the Ganga's patience.

The city swallowed him in its labyrinth of alleys. The smell of fried *kachoris* curled from a stall, a man sang a bhajan in a voice roughened by age, and above it all, the constant murmur of the river seemed to follow him, even when he could no longer see her.

That night, Sid slept in a *dharamshala* near the ghats. In his dreams, the Ganga appeared again—not as water, but as a great silver thread weaving its way through mountains, forests, and cities. Wherever it passed, people's faces softened, their voices lowered, and the land grew green.

When he woke, the dream stayed with him like the taste of water after thirst.

To hold on to peace, you must learn to let everything else go.

DSN

Chapter Five – The Monk of Bodh Gaya

The road from Varanasi to Bodh Gaya felt different from every path Sid had walked so far.

It was neither the restless shifting of the desert dunes nor the crowded hum of a bazaar street. This road seemed to move at its own pace, slow but certain, lined with banyan trees whose roots hung like patient hands waiting for the right moment to touch the earth.

From the moment he left the ghats, the river's murmur lingered in his ears. But with each day's walk southward, that murmur faded, replaced by another sound. Silence. Not the hollow silence of an empty place, but a silence with weight, as though something in the air was listening.

Bodh Gaya announced itself not with noise, but with stillness. The Mahabodhi Temple rose before him, its carved spire piercing the sky like an arrow aimed at heaven. Around it, pilgrims from every corner of the world moved in quiet devotion—Tibetan monks in maroon robes spinning prayer wheels, Burmese nuns in pale pink chanting softly, Indian villagers with folded hands offering marigold garlands at the temple gates.

Sid felt suddenly out of place in his worn desert kurta and dust-covered sandals. But no one seemed to notice him as anything but another traveller. Here, everyone's footprints blended into the same earth.

The Bodhi tree stood to the left of the temple courtyard, its wide branches shading the spot where, centuries ago, a prince named Siddhartha had sat until he found the thing every seeker chases and every wanderer names differently—enlightenment, freedom, shanti.

The tree's leaves trembled in the light breeze, catching the sun so that they seemed to glow. Pilgrims sat in circles beneath it, meditating in perfect stillness. Sid watched them, wondering how anyone could sit so long without twitching or scratching an itch.

He was about to turn away when a voice spoke behind him.

"You are staring like a man who wants to sit, but fears he will fall asleep."

Sid turned. The speaker was a monk of indeterminate age—his head shaved, his skin bronze, his eyes holding a depth that made Sid feel suddenly transparent.

"I don't know if I can sit like that," Sid admitted.

The monk smiled faintly. "Then perhaps you should try."

He gestured toward an empty mat beneath the tree. Sid hesitated. The fakir had sent him across deserts and cities; the merchant had taught him patience; the dervishes had shown him surrender; the boatman had shown him impermanence. Maybe stillness was the next step.

He sat.

The monk settled beside him. "Close your eyes," he said. "Listen to the sound of your breath. When thoughts come, let them pass, like clouds over the desert sky you know so well."

Sid did as he was told. At first, his mind wandered—thinking of the gold spool in his pouch, of the Ganga's murmur, of whether his camels were still safe back home. His legs began to ache, his back protested, and his eyelids twitched against the temptation to peek.

The monk's voice was steady. "This is not about stopping thoughts. It is about not following them when they run."

Time blurred. The heat of the afternoon softened into the coolness of evening. Sid's breathing slowed, and for the first time in years, he felt no urge to be anywhere but here. The ache in his legs remained, but it no longer demanded his attention.

When he opened his eyes, the courtyard was bathed in the gold of the setting sun. The monk beside him was still sitting, as still as the carved pillars of the temple.

"You stayed longer than most on their first attempt," the monk said, opening his eyes at last. "What did you see?"

Sid thought for a moment. "I saw my thoughts trying to pull me away, but I didn't follow. It felt like … keeping my seat on a camel that wanted to bolt."

The monk laughed softly. "Yes. That is the first victory—staying where you are when everything tries to move you."

Over the next three days, Sid returned each morning to sit beneath the Bodhi tree. The silence began to feel less like an empty room and more like a full cup. He noticed things he would have missed before: the way the light shifted across the temple's carvings, the exact sound of a leaf falling on stone, the smell of incense before the first prayer was spoken.

On the fourth day, the monk handed him a small piece of coarse cotton cloth. "Keep this," he said.

Sid unfolded it. Inside was a single Bodhi leaf, dried to a perfect skeleton, its veins forming a delicate network that seemed too fragile to have survived.

"This is a reminder," the monk said, "that stillness is not the absence of movement—it is the foundation from which movement can grow without shaking."

Before leaving Bodh Gaya, Sid placed the leaf carefully in his pouch alongside the gold spool and the fakir's couplet. The pouch now held not just objects, but lessons—patience, surrender, impermanence, and now, stillness.

As he stepped back onto the road, the monk called after him, "Remember—peace is not found by reaching the end of the path, but by being fully present for every step along it."

Sid turned, bowed, and continued walking. The leaf's lightness seemed to balance the weight of his journey so far.

That night, as he camped under a tamarind tree, Sid felt no rush to reach the next place. For the first time since leaving the desert, the road itself felt like home.

Stillness is the root from which all journeys draw their strength.

DSN

Chapter Six – The Weaver of the Clouds

The road north from Bodh Gaya was different from anything Sid had travelled so far.

The flat lands slowly tilted upward, the air grew thinner, and the horizon became jagged with the teeth of the Himalayas. Villages here were sparse, clinging to the slopes like stubborn shrubs. The people spoke in clipped syllables that carried the rhythm of mountain streams.

The gold spool, the fakir's couplet, and the Bodhi leaf travelled with him now like three quiet companions. Each had its own weight and story. And yet, he felt a thread missing—the actual thread of shanti that the fakir had promised.

Days turned into a week as Sid followed the trail deeper into the hills. At night, he slept under pine trees whose needles whispered secrets to the wind. He learned to walk in silence, for even his own breathing seemed to echo in the valleys.

One evening, as the sun dipped behind a snow-shouldered peak, he saw smoke curling from a distant ridge. It was not the thick, hurried smoke of cooking fires but a slow, deliberate column, like incense rising from a single stick.

He followed it.

The path wound upward, narrow, and uneven. A single misstep would send him tumbling into the gorge below. His legs burned, his breath grew ragged, but the smoke pulled him on like a thread that would not let him go.

At last, he reached a flat clearing where a small stone house stood, its roof weighted with slabs to keep the wind from lifting it away. In front of the house sat an old woman, her back straight despite the years carved into it. Her hair was a waterfall of white, tied in a long braid. She worked a wooden loom, her hands moving with such grace that Sid felt he was watching a dance.

The cloth she wove shimmered, though it was not silk. Threads of pale blue, soft green, and golden-yellow ran together in patterns that seemed to shift when he looked too long. Beside her sat baskets of wildflowers—their petals crushed into bowls of dye.

The woman looked up without surprise, as though she had been expecting him.

"You've walked far," she said. Her voice was the sound of rain on leaves—soft, but impossible to ignore.

Sid stepped closer. "I … I think I've been looking for you."

She smiled faintly. "And I, perhaps, for you."

She gestured for him to sit. The loom creaked softly as her shuttle moved back and forth. "Do you know what I am weaving?" she asked.

"It looks like a shawl," Sid said.

"It is more than that. Each thread carries a season, a wind, a prayer whispered to the clouds." She paused to lift a strand of pale yellow. "This is dyed from marigolds that grew where a family reconciled after years of silence. This blue comes from flowers gathered after the first rains ended a drought. This green is from leaves given by a tree that survived a lightning strike."

Sid watched, mesmerised. "You weave stories," he said.

"I weave what the world gives me," she replied. "And when the cloth is finished, it carries a piece of peace. Those who wrap themselves in it remember something they thought they had lost."

He told her about the fakir, the prophecy, the river, the merchant, the dervishes, the monk. She listened without interrupting, her hands never stopping their work.

When he finished, she nodded. "You've gathered all the colours, all the lessons. Now they must be woven together."

"I don't know how," Sid admitted.

"You do," she said gently. "Peace is not something you find whole. It is something you gather together from what life has already given you."

She showed him how to hold the shuttle, how to feed the thread through without pulling too hard. "If you pull in haste, the thread snaps. If you hold back, the pattern is loose. You must give it just enough tension to keep it strong, and just enough slack to let it breathe."

For hours they worked side by side. Sid added a strand of gold from his spool, the one Viren had given him. She smiled at the shimmer it brought to the cloth. "Every pattern needs light," she said. "Light reminds the darkness it cannot stay forever."

When the weaving was done, she cut the cloth from the loom and placed it in his lap. It was lighter than he expected, yet warm, as if it held the memory of every hand, every place, and every season it had touched.

"This," she said, "is the *thread of shanti* the fakir spoke of. But remember—it is not just this cloth.

It is the patience of the merchant, the surrender of the dervish, the letting-go of the river, the stillness of the monk, and the colours of the world you carried here. Without those, this is only a thread."

Sid looked at the cloth and understood. The journey had not been about finding something to take back; it had been about gathering pieces of himself he had left scattered in other places.

The woman wrapped the cloth carefully and handed it to him. "When you return to your village, teach them what you have learned. Weave with them, not for them. That is how peace stays."

As he left the clearing, the old woman returned to her loom. The shuttle moved again, and the sound of it followed him down the mountain like a heartbeat.

Peace is woven from many threads—patience, surrender, letting go, stillness, and light.

DSN

Chapter Seven – The Loom Within

The mountains let Sid go the way elders bless a departing child—quietly, with a hand raised and eyes that have already forgiven the distance. He descended through belts of pine and rhododendron, through villages where prayer flags wrote soft sentences across the wind.

The cloth the old woman had given him lay folded against his chest, warm as a kept promise. In his pouch, the gold spool from Viren and the Bodhi leaf rested beside the fakir's couplet. The four objects no longer felt separate; together they beat like a small, steady heart.

When the ranges flattened and the air grew heavier with dust, he knew he was close to home. The desert did not look different for his having left it; dunes do not rehearse for returns. But he did. His step was slower, the kind of slow that was not tiredness but care—each footfall a word he chose rather than blurted.

From the last rise before the village, he saw the familiar: the ring of mud houses, the thorn fences, the single khejri tree that had once been his only roof. He also saw what absence had sharpened: a well whose stone mouth had whitened with thirst; a line of women carrying empty vessels that made no hopeful music; men speaking with their hands because anger never trusts its voice.

He entered without announcement. A child saw him first, children always do, and ran ahead shouting his name. Heads turned. Some faces warmed, some did not. A boy who leaves is a story; a boy who returns is an answer people are not sure they want.

His father stepped out of a doorway, thinner, hair crowded with grey. The two stood a breath apart, then closed the distance like drawing a stitch—one in, one out, pull gently, and let the cloth remember it is whole.

"You came back," his father said, as if reporting the weather.

"I learned how," Sid replied, and the older man, who had learned to measure love in unsent letters, nodded.

They ate in silence that evening: coarse rotis, an onion split cleanly, water measured into metal cups as if it were an expensive spice. After, Sid spread the cloth on the floor. The room filled with a light that was not brightness but presence—the kind that lets shadows stay without making them powerful.

"What is it?" his father asked.

"A way to remember peace," Sid said. "And a way to practice it."

Practice was not a word the village had used with peace before.

The next morning, Sid took the cloth to the square and called the people. They came from habit; in drought, any summons might be a ration. He did not stand on the raised plinth where news and blame were usually traded. He sat on the ground beside the cloth and waited until the village remembered how to listen without being told.

"I walked across cities and rivers and mountains," he said when the quiet grew sturdy, "not to bring you a miracle, but to bring you a loom."

There was a murmur, patient at first, then bristling. "We need water," someone said. "We need rain," said another. "We need traders to buy our animals," said a third. Needs become a chorus when people forget they can sing other songs.

Sid held up the gold spool. "This is patience," he said. "You cannot drink it. But without it, the well will not rise."

He lifted the Bodhi leaf. "This is stillness. You cannot plant it. But without it, our anger will trample seedlings as if they were weeds."

He touched the cloth. "This is surrender. Not to fate, but to each other—to the work that must be done with more hands than we have used so far."

"And the rain?" a woman asked, her voice tired in a way that had nothing to do with sleep.

"The rain is a guest," Sid said. "We have been arguing about whether it will visit. We have not cleaned the house."

They did not understand, which is to say they understood enough to be irritated. A man with a voice trained by quarrels stepped forward. "Words are a poor ration," he said. "What will you do?"

Sid did not answer with a speech. He answered with a rope.

He walked to the old well and tied the rope to the stone ring, then to the khejri tree. "We will lower stone by stone," he said. "We will shore the mouth. We will line the inside with the broken pots we never threw away, because broken things can still be useful.

"We will call the women to measure where shade falls, and build the windbreaks where they say, because they know the wind better than men who chase it. We will sink percolation pits beyond the dunes and stitch them with brush. We will learn the river's manners and bow to the mountain we cannot move by moving what we can."

There was a silence. Then someone laughed—a short, surprised sound that did not belong to scorn. Work has a way of shaming cynicism simply by beginning.

They worked. The first day, badly. Men shouted instructions they did not understand. Children ran in helpful circles. The rope burned palms that had mostly known the weight of arguments. By evening, the well looked exactly like itself, only more tired.

At night, Sid unrolled the cloth in the square. He asked them to sit around it, not as spectators but as a circle that could nearly touch. He told them of the merchant who taught him to pull thread like breathing, not like yanking a stubborn goat. He told them of the dervishes who turned until the self had set down its weapons. He told them of the boatman whose river never held anything for longer than a moment and yet was never empty. He told them of the monk who said sitting is the bravest motion.

He did not preach. He narrated. Stories are tools polite enough to use in public.

On the second day, the rope no longer slipped. On the third, the first ring of stones seated itself like a word that finally finds its sentence. Women placed their palms on the well's lip before lowering their pails—with permission, not petition. Children brought broken pots, proud of their sudden wealth. The old men argued about angles and then laughed because the rope insisted on a different truth.

In the heat of the fourth afternoon, a boy slipped. Sid caught him by the wrist and held on until the panic remembered it had feet. When they sat to breathe, the boy pointed at the cloth. "It shines," he said.

"It remembers," Sid corrected, and realised he was speaking to himself.

On the seventh day, the wind changed. It came from the direction of the old riverbed that only the oldest women spoke of, lowering their voices as if the river were sleeping and should not be woken rudely. Dust rose, yes, but with it a smell that made spines straighten: petrichor's first letter written somewhere out of sight.

Clouds gathered like guests approaching a gate, deciding whether to enter. The village, which had forgotten how to be a host, offered what it could—quiet. Even the goats, habitual complainers, went still.

The first drop struck the cloth.

It did not soak in. It rested, a bright bead on the woven surface, then rolled toward a warp of gold and vanished into the pattern as if admitted to a small, private heaven. Another drop. Then another. The cloth did not drink greedily. It received the water like an elder receives a visitor, with respect and an unhurried smile.

The rain came in a good temper. Not a rage, not a sulk. A measured, persuading rain that talked to the earth until it agreed to listen. The well's new stones darkened. The rope grew heavy. The first bucket came up brimming, and no one cheered. They did not have breath for noise. They drank as if remembering how.

Sid stepped back, letting the circle fill itself. He looked for his father and found him standing at the edge, eyes refusing the easy permission of tears. They nodded, the way men nod when something simpler than pride is doing the speaking.

That night, the village did not sleep. The rain softened to a whisper and the square became a loom. Sid showed them how to stretch warp between two pegs, how to beat weft gently, how to keep the thread from sulking. Women showed him how to sit so a back remembers its future. Children threaded beads into borders that had room for clumsy beauty. The cloth grew, not into a single garment but into a practice the hands could carry even when the cloth itself was away being worn.

They wove not only with thread. They wove with the way they handed a cup, with the way they paused before replying, with the way they left a door unlatched for a neighbour who had once latched his heart. The village's grammar changed: from nouns of possession to verbs of attention.

Word spread the way water does—quietly ambitious. A caravan halted for a midday rest and stayed two days. A woman from the next village arrived with a quarrel and left with a shawl that made her quarrel forget why it had come. A moneylender walked through by mistake and forgave a debt he could not remember hating. Not magic; practice.

One afternoon, a group from a far town brought a torn wedding sari. "The border split in the jostle," they said, embarrassed as if the cloth had chosen to betray them. Sid examined it and nodded toward the circle. "Sit," he said, "and tell the story of the wedding while we mend."

They spoke, and as they spoke, hands moved. The tear closed as steadily as a wound that knows it is already forgiven. When they left, the sari shone at the seam, gold brighter where it had once been broken. Someone whispered, "You cannot unsee the joining."

A month into the weaving, the fakir came.

Not to be recognised, though a few did. He leaned on his staff beneath the khejri and watched without interfering, the smile of a messenger who has found the right doorstep. Sid saw him and went to him and placed the clay cup in his palm.

"You kept it empty," the fakir said, approving.

"It kept me," Sid replied.

They walked to the well together. The fakir peered in, then looked up at the sky as if comparing shades of blue. "You have a good rope," he said.

"We took turns holding it," Sid said.

"Ah," the fakir said, "so no one's hands burned for long."

He touched the cloth. "This is not the thing I promised," he said softly. "It is better. Promises end at their words. Practice begins where words are shy."

They sat at the edge of the square while evening divided the light into keep and give. "What will you do when the rains forget you again?" the fakir asked.

"We will remember each other," Sid said. "And each remembering will be a kind of water."

The fakir closed his eyes, as a man does when he thanks without wanting witnesses. When he opened them, they were full of road. "I will go," he said, "before the village learns my face and tries to keep me. I am good at many things; staying is not one of them."

"Teach me one more couplet," Sid said, grinning.

The fakir thought, then shook his head. "No. Today is for prose." He rose, raised his staff toward the well, toward the cloth, toward the circle that had learned to treat silence like a guest, and walked into the dusk until the dusk folded him.

By the time the fields remembered green and the goats forgot to complain, the cloth had a name it had not asked for: the Weaver's Shawl. Mothers draped it over children with fevers. Men wore it to settle arguments the way rain settles dust. It did not cure or decide; it reminded. Of what? Of quiet, mostly. Of the first step that is far. Of the second that is easy. Of the third that feels like a promise to someone you cannot yet name.

Sid did not become a priest or a chief. He became what the village had not known it needed: a keeper of pace. He rang no bell, yet work started when he stood and paused when he sat. He spoke softly, so people had to lean in, and in leaning, discovered they had already moved toward each other.

Sometimes, at dusk, he walked to the ridge and looked toward the horizon that had once rehearsed for him. He did not feel trapped. He felt threaded. The road was still there, as available as breath, and perhaps he would take it again. But the loom within him no longer needed distance to work.

On a morning when the light had the taste of milk, he found the boy he had once saved from slipping at the well practicing with the shuttle. The boy's tongue peeked between his lips, full of concentration. "Like this?" he asked, beating a line too hard.

"Like this," Sid said, loosening the hand with one finger, the way one loosens a knot that has begun to trust.

The pattern evened. The boy grinned. "It listens," he said, surprised.

"They always do," Sid replied. "Threads. People. Even wells."

He looked at the cloth on the square. It had been mended many times, not because it tore easily, but because the village handled it often. Its gold caught the morning and gave it back without keeping interest.

The loom inside him thrummed, a low, constant sound like a contented beast. He understood the fakir's first lesson finally—not as poetry, but as instruction: *Carry emptiness without being empty.*

He did. The cup was light in his pouch. His hands were light at their work. The village was lighter than its history.

He tied the rope to the bucket and lowered it until the well's cool mouth drank. When he pulled, the water came up willing. He looked into its skin and saw, not his face, but the pattern of the sky resting there, unafraid.

He smiled and carried the bucket toward the square where a circle had already formed, where a shuttle waited for the day to begin its gentle argument with thread.

A village learns peace when its people learn each other's pace.

DSN

Chapter Eight – The Well of Shanti

The desert had a long memory, but it did not often share it. It kept its own records—in the lean of a dune, in the way the khejri tree's roots found water no one could see, in the small shifts of wind that only the oldest herders noticed. When Sid returned from his journey years ago, the desert did not greet him as a prodigal son. It simply allowed him to stay.

The seasons had come and gone since then—good rains, reluctant rains, dry years that tested tempers and patient years that mended them. The village had changed in ways that were both visible and invisible.

The well had been rebuilt stone by stone; its walls lined with the pottery shards of those who had once argued over them. The square had grown used to the sound of the shuttle passing from hand to hand. And the shawl—the Weaver's Shawl—was no longer a novelty; it was a part of the village's grammar, like greetings at the morning market or the taste of the first mango in summer.

***

The cloth had travelled further than Sid. It had been worn at weddings, laid gently over new mothers, wrapped around the shoulders of grieving fathers.

It had gone to markets in distant towns and returned with the smell of incense from other shrines. Once, it had even gone to a nearby desert fair, where a camel trader asked to borrow it to settle a dispute over grazing land; when the shawl was laid between the two men, their voices softened without knowing why.

But perhaps the greatest change was not in the cloth, but in the people. The act of weaving had stitched patience into their days. Disputes were no longer resolved by whose voice was loudest, but by who was willing to sit the longest in the circle, letting their hands find the rhythm of the loom. The desert's silence, once a thing to be endured, had become a resource.

***

One early morning, as the sun rose like a shy coin in the east, a caravan from the north arrived—camels draped in bells, carts laden with grain and bright cloth. Among the traders was a young man with nimble fingers and a nervous smile.

"Are you the weaver?" he asked Sid in the square.

"I am one of them," Sid replied. "Here, many weave."

The young man's eyes lit up when Sid invited him to sit in the circle. He carried with him a small pouch from Ahmedabad. Inside was a spool of gold thread and a letter in Viren's neat hand:

Patience, like cloth, must be renewed. I send you more light to weave into the dark.

Sid held the spool for a moment, feeling the familiar weight. The light from Viren's shop seemed to travel in it still.

A week later, a young dervish from Ajmer came walking into the square, robes dusted from travel. He bowed slightly and said, "I have turned with the wind long enough. Now I wish to turn with the thread."

Not long after, a boy from Varanasi arrived, sent by the boatman's apprentice. He brought a jar of Ganga water, sealed tight. "The boatman said to tell you: don't knot it too tight, even if it's sacred," the boy said with a grin.

These were not mere visits—they were the river, the bazaar, and the whirling dance coming back to the desert, one footstep at a time.

***

That year, the rains came early, and the village decided to hold the first Festival of Threads. For three days, people wove in the square from dawn until the stars outshone the oil lamps. Families brought their own threads—dyed in colours from their homes: turmeric yellows, indigo blues, rust reds from crushed stones, green from desert herbs.

One woman contributed strands from an old sari her mother had worn the day she was married. A boy added a strip cut from the hem of a festival kurta. Even travellers were invited to add something from their journey. The loom did not mind if the threads were uneven or frayed; it accepted them all, weaving them into a whole no one could have planned.

Music filled the air—dholak beats, reed flutes, and the low hum of songs that had travelled from other villages. Food stalls appeared as if summoned—flatbreads puffing over clay stoves, sweets dusted with cardamom, sherbet cooling in earthen pots. Laughter carried itself through everything.

On the final night, the shawl was not hung as a relic but worn, passed from shoulder to shoulder, so that every person carried its warmth for a moment. When it came to Sid, he wrapped it around himself and looked at the circle—faces lit by lamp and starlight, hands stained with dye, eyes softened by the work they had done together.

***

It was on the last evening of the festival that Sid saw him—leaning on his brass-ringed staff under the khejri tree, the red bundle slung across his back. The fakir looked older, but the desert dust on his kurta was the same.

Sid crossed the square. "You came back."

"I never left," the fakir said. "The wind kept me here in its stories."

They sat together, watching the weaving circle. "You found the thread," the fakir said.

"We found it," Sid corrected.

The fakir smiled. "And now?"

"Now we keep weaving," Sid said. "And teach others to weave."

"Good," the fakir said. "But remember—threads are for joining, not for binding. One day, you will have to carry this beyond the dunes."

Sid nodded. "When the time is right."

The fakir reached into his bundle and handed Sid a scrap of cloth. "This is for your next journey. No prophecy this time. Only practice."

***

The next morning, the festival ended with a final act. The shawl was laid flat in the square, and with the agreement of all, it was cut into several pieces. Each family took one to keep, to use, to wear—not as an heirloom to guard, but as a living piece of work. One larger square remained in the centre of the village, on the same loom where it had begun.

Sid tied Viren's gold thread into its border. The young dervish added a tassel dyed in the colour of evening sky. The boy from Varanasi dipped one edge in Ganga water before it dried in the desert sun.

The shawl, smaller now but more present than ever, caught the light, and the gold thread shimmered as though nodding in approval.

That night, as the desert cooled and the stars came out sharp and near, Sid walked to the ridge outside the village. The horizon lay open and patient. Somewhere beyond it, other villages waited—places where wells still ran dry, where tempers outpaced patience, where the loom within had not yet been found.

He knew he would go. Not tomorrow, not next month—but soon. And when he did, he would carry the gold spool, the Bodhi leaf, the scrap from the fakir, and, most importantly, the habit of weaving peace—one patient thread at a time.

The wind rose gently, lifting the edge of his kurta. It carried the faintest scent of rain, though no clouds were in sight. Sid smiled. The wind had always known his name.

The true thread of peace is not in the cloth, but in the hands that keep passing it on.

DSN

II

Chapter Nine – The Call Beyond the Desert

The desert, for all its stillness, is a place of movement. Winds travel without borders, caravans cross with rumours strapped to their saddles, and news often arrives long before the people who carry it.

It was just past midday when the first sign came. Sid was at the loom in the square, showing two young women how to ease a stubborn thread without snapping it, when the shadow of a camel fell across the work.

He looked up to see a trader he half-recognised—thin as a bowstring, his beard full of dust, his eyes scanning the square with the urgency of someone searching for water.

"Are you Sid, of the Well of Shanti?" the trader asked.

Sid nodded.

The trader dismounted slowly, as though the news he carried was heavier than the sacks tied to his saddle. "I have come from Kherapur," he said. "It lies eight days to the west, beyond the salt flats. The rains have not visited them for three years. The wells are dead. People are … forgetting how to speak to each other without shouting."

Sid understood the danger in those words. A dry well could be dug deeper; a dry heart was harder to reach.

The trader pulled a small bundle from his pack. Inside was a torn piece of cloth—plain cotton, worn thin at the edges. But in one corner, faint and fraying, was a single golden thread.

"It came to us with a group of shepherds," the trader explained. "They said it was part of a larger cloth, from a village where people had learned to work together. They told of a man who taught them to weave not only fabric, but peace. We found this scrap in our storehouse. Some of us believe if you made the cloth, you can teach us to make another. Others think it is foolishness. I … think it is worth the risk of the journey."

Sid took the scrap in his hands. The gold thread caught the sunlight, dim but still holding its shimmer, as though it had been waiting to be recognised. He turned it over, feeling the roughness where it had torn away.

The square was quiet now, the weaving paused. People watched with the same attentive stillness they had shown the first time he unrolled The Weaver's Shawl years ago.

"What will you do?" asked the young dervish, who had stayed in the village since the Festival of Threads.

Sid looked around the circle—at the faces of those who had learned to pull thread gently, to speak in turns, to work without keeping score. "We will go," he said.

That night, the village gathered under the khejri tree. The shawl's central piece lay across the loom, a square of worn beauty mended so many times that its repairs were part of its pattern. Sid placed the torn scrap from Kherapur beside it.

"The thread we have here," he told them, "is not meant to stay in one place. When a well is full, we draw water for others. When a loom is strong, we use it to mend what lies beyond our own roof."

They began to prepare without being told. The young boy from the caravan oiled the loom's joints so it could travel. The women measured and wound spools of cotton dyed in colours they thought might carry hope—sunrise yellow, raincloud grey, the green of desert herbs after a storm. The children packed the shawl's offcuts, the Bodhi leaf, and the gold spool that Viren had sent.

Before dawn, Sid stood at the edge of the village with the young dervish, the caravan boy, and two women who had woven the most hours over the past year. The trader from Kherapur waited with his camel, a second animal carrying the loom, wrapped in cloth to keep the dust from its hinges.

The fakir appeared, as if the wind had carried him there. He looked at the bundle on the second camel, then at Sid. "You are leaving," he said.

Sid smiled. "The thread is ready."

The fakir placed his brass-ringed staff in Sid's hands. "This time, the road may be longer than you think. Take this. It remembers more paths than your feet do."

As they set out, the village walked with them to the first rise. From there, the square, the well, and the khejri tree were all visible in one glance. Sid turned to look one last time—not in farewell, but as a weaver checks his first row before beginning the second.

The wind rose, warm and steady, tugging at his kurta. It smelled faintly of marigold and rain, as though carrying blessings from every place he had been.

"Eight days," the trader said, adjusting the strap of his pack.

"Eight days," Sid replied. Then he began to walk, the gold thread of the Kherapur scrap tucked into his pouch beside the Bodhi leaf, Viren's spool, and the fakir's couplet. The desert stretched ahead, vast and waiting.

Somewhere beyond the salt flats, another loom stood empty.

When a well is full, draw water for others. When peace is strong, carry it where it is needed most.

Chapter Ten – Across the Salt Flats

The desert ends in its own time.

For days, Sid and his companions walked through sand that shifted beneath their feet, dunes folding and unfolding like restless blankets. Then, without warning, the gold of the dunes gave way to a white glare that stung the eyes.

The salt flats stretched before them—vast, unbroken, shimmering like a frozen sea. Here, the air held no scent of herbs or dung fires, only the faint tang of salt and sun. The horizon was a straight line, unsoftened by trees or hills, and the silence was so complete it made their own breathing feel loud.

The caravan moved in single file. The trader from Kherapur led the way, his camel's bells muffled to avoid spooking the animals on the barren ground. Behind him came the two women from Sid's village, their spools of dyed thread strapped to their packs, followed by the young dervish, the caravan boy, and finally Sid, walking beside the second camel that carried the loom.

Each morning, they started before the sun's edge broke the horizon, using the cooler hours to cover distance. By midday, the glare was so intense they wrapped their heads in cloth and walked with eyes narrowed to slits. In the evenings, they camped where the salt crust was thick enough to hold the pegs of their tents, though the wind often had other ideas.

The salt flats were a place without reference points. Distances lied. What seemed a short walk could take hours; what looked far might be reached before they realised, they had been walking toward it. It was here that Sid remembered the monk's voice beneath the Bodhi tree: *The first victory is staying where you are when everything tries to move you.*

The stillness was deceptive. The salt shifted under their steps, crunching in a way that made them constantly aware of the ground's fragility. The trader warned them never to stray from the path—beneath the crust, the flats could hide pools of brine deep enough to swallow a camel.

On the fourth day, they met their first challenge. One of the loom's bindings came loose from the camel's saddle, the wooden frame twisting awkwardly with each step. Sid and the young dervish stopped to adjust it, but the knot kept slipping.

"Pull tighter," the boy suggested.

Sid shook his head. "Too tight, and it will snap. Too loose, and it will sway. The loom is no different from thread."

They worked together, finding the right tension. When it held, Sid smiled—Viren's lesson was alive in his hands.

That night, as the moon turned the salt flats into a silver mirror, they sat in a circle outside their tents. The two women began weaving a small strip of cloth using the travel loom—nothing fancy, just plain cotton, but the act steadied their minds after a day of glare and emptiness.

The young dervish asked, "What will we do in Kherapur if they don't trust us?"

"Then we will weave first," Sid said. "And speak after. A pattern is harder to refuse once it's begun."

On the sixth day, they saw signs of life again—scrub grass, a lone thorn tree, and the faint shape of distant hills. But the final stretch was the hardest. The wind picked up, blowing fine salt into their faces, stinging their eyes and lips. They walked with heads bowed, following the sound of the trader's bells more than the sight of him.

When they finally reached the edge of the flats, the ground turned to firm, cracked earth. The trader stopped and pointed westward. "Kherapur is two days from here. The wells are dry, and tempers are shorter than the walk you've just made. But they will listen to a story if you tell it with your hands."

Sid looked out toward the horizon. Somewhere beyond it lay a village that had forgotten the loom within. He touched the pouch at his side—the gold thread, the Bodhi leaf, the torn scrap from Kherapur itself.

"Then we'll weave them one," he said.

They made camp at the edge of the flats. That night, Sid couldn't sleep. The salt stretched behind them like a completed row on the loom, and ahead, he could almost feel the next row waiting.

He remembered the fakir's staff in his hand and the weight of the words the old woman in the mountains had told him: *Weave with them, not for them.* It was not a warning; it was a promise.

When the morning came, they would step into Kherapur together—not as saviours, but as weavers of a cloth the village could claim as its own.

Some patterns can only be woven after crossing empty spaces.

DSN

Chapter Eleven — Kherapur's Fractures

They reached Kherapur on the morning of the second day after leaving the salt flats. The village was not what Sid expected. From a distance, it looked almost prosperous—flat-roofed houses of baked mud, courtyards shaded by neem and tamarind, a cluster of stalls selling jaggery, lentils, and goat's milk. But as they walked deeper into the lanes, the cracks began to show.

The air was heavy with the sour scent of stale water. At the first well, a line of women waited, their brass pots resting on hips and heads, the line silent except for the sound of shifting feet. The water that trickled from the spout was brown, and the women's eyes slid over strangers without welcome.

The trader led them to a small square where an old banyan tree cast its shade. The square should have been a place for markets and gossip, but it was nearly empty. Two men sat on opposite sides, sharpening sickles without looking at each other. The tension was almost physical, like the moment before cloth tears.

Sid noticed other signs: two weaving sheds, both in disrepair, on opposite sides of the square. Looms stood idle, their frames dry and warped. Threads hung from nails on the wall, knotted and tangled.

"What happened here?" Sid asked quietly.

The trader sighed. "They split. Over the last harvest, over the water, over who should repair the wells first.

Families stopped speaking. The two weaving groups stopped trading cloth. Even the children are told not to play across the street."

The young dervish whispered, "How do you teach peace to people who won't even greet each other?"

Sid didn't answer right away. Instead, he walked to the banyan's trunk, placed his palm against it, and let the quiet sink into him. He remembered the monk's lesson under the Bodhi tree: *Do not begin with what is broken. Begin with what they still share.*

When he turned back, his eyes rested on the two weaving sheds. "We will start with thread," he said.

They approached the first shed. Inside, a group of women sat with baskets of raw cotton, their conversation clipped and cautious. Sid knelt beside the oldest among them, a woman whose hair was more silver than black, and placed in her lap the scrap of cloth from Kherapur with the single gold thread.

"This thread came from here," he said. "It's waiting for its cloth to be whole again."

She looked at the scrap for a long time before speaking. "And who will weave with us? Them?" She tilted her chin toward the shed across the square.

Sid shook his head. "For now, me."

That afternoon, Sid and his companions set up the travelling loom in the middle of the square, between the two sheds. It was a deliberate choice—neither side's territory, but in the open where anyone could see. The loom's polished wood caught the sun, and the bright spools from his village glowed against the dusty ground.

At first, only a few women from the first shed came forward. Sid showed them how to tension the warp, letting them handle the gold thread so they could feel its strength. Slowly, passersby stopped to watch. Children gathered first, whispering, then some of the younger men, drawn by curiosity if not goodwill.

From across the square, a boy from the second shed approached. He stood for a while, arms crossed, then blurted, "You're doing it wrong."

Sid smiled. "Then show me."

The boy hesitated, then came forward, his fingers quick and sure as he adjusted the shuttle's path. A woman from the second shed came to call him back, but instead of leaving, she stood watching, her hands twitching as if they missed the feel of thread.

By sunset, a narrow strip of cloth had begun to grow on the loom. It was imperfect—some loose wefts, a few uneven lines—but it was something made together, in the same place, at the same time.

As they covered the loom for the night, the young dervish said, "That was just one day. They still won't speak to each other."

Sid nodded. "Peace isn't stitched in a day. But today, they touched the same cloth."

That night, as the village lights flickered, Sid lay awake, listening to the faint hum of looms from both sheds. Somewhere in the darkness, the gold thread gleamed under the moonlight, waiting for the next row.

Begin where the threads can still meet, and the rest will follow.

DSN

Chapter Twelve – The Loom Between Two Wells

Morning in Kherapur began with the sound of brass pots clanging at the wells. One stood at the north end of the square, the other at the south. The space between them—thirty paces at most—was a no-man's land. Women from the north well would not step past the banyan tree; women from the south well refused to come closer than the shadow it cast.

Sid had seen wars fought over boundaries wider than this. And yet, here was a division so small it could be crossed in twenty heartbeats, but so deep that generations had been swallowed by it.

On the second day after setting up the loom, Sid woke before sunrise. The square was empty except for the trader, who was heating water for tea, and the young dervish, who had taken to sleeping near the loom to "guard it from wandering goats."

Sid walked to the banyan tree and placed the loom directly in the centre—so that the front end faced the north well and the back end faced the south. No one could approach it without stepping into that unspoken territory between.

When the first women came for water, they stopped at their usual invisible lines. A few pretended not to notice the loom. Others stood, watching in silence as Sid and the dervish began the morning's weaving.

By mid-morning, a boy from the south well wandered over, holding a brass pot almost as big as his torso. He stared at the warp threads, fascinated. Sid beckoned him closer.

"Do you want to try?" Sid asked.

The boy nodded but looked over his shoulder. His grandmother, standing near the well, tightened her lips and gave the smallest shake of her head. Sid pretended not to see and handed the boy the shuttle anyway.

The boy passed it once, clumsily, before his grandmother called him back. But in those few seconds, the cloth had grown by one imperfect, golden line.

By the third day, something shifted. A woman from the north well came forward to examine the loom. She didn't sit, didn't speak, just watched for several minutes before leaving. In the afternoon, a young man from the south side brought a bundle of dyed cotton. "Waste from our shed," he said gruffly, dropping it near the loom. "You can use it if you want."

The women from the north well glanced at it, sniffed, and said nothing—but that evening, the same cotton appeared woven into the cloth, its deep indigo standing out against the gold and cream.

On the fifth day, Sid began a new pattern—an interlocking motif he had learned from the monk's temple, one that could not be completed without alternating colours from two different sources. He didn't explain the symbolism. He just asked for more thread.

By the end of the week, they had to fetch thread from both sheds to keep the pattern alive. The act of passing spools across the square was awkward at first—hands avoiding direct touch, eyes looking anywhere but at the person opposite—but the threads moved nonetheless.

The wells themselves became part of the weaving. Sid suggested rinsing the newly woven strips in fresh water to tighten the fibres. But neither well's water alone was enough to rinse the growing cloth without staining it.

So, they did something unthinkable: they filled two pots—one from each well—and poured them together into a large basin. The water swirled into a pale, clear blend. Someone joked that the cloth would now belong to both sides. No one laughed aloud, but no one disagreed either.

One evening, as the sun dipped low, Sid noticed something: children from both sides were sitting under the banyan, chasing each other around the loom while their mothers wove. The no-man's land was now a playground.

The young dervish leaned toward Sid and whispered, "The wells will be the last thing to change."

Sid smiled faintly. "No. They've already begun. The water is mixing. It just doesn't know it yet."

That night, they left the loom uncovered, trusting that no one would harm what had begun to belong to everyone. The gold thread glimmered in the moonlight, now surrounded by indigo, crimson, and soft cream—colours that had once lived apart, now locked in a single, unbreakable weave.

Peace begins when the water from two wells is poured into the same vessel.

DSN

Chapter Thirteen — The Pattern That Spoke

By the second week, the cloth stretched nearly to the length of a sleeping cow. It swayed gently in the Kherapur wind, catching the light in a way that made it seem alive.

At first glance, it was only colours—gold, indigo, crimson, and cream—but when the morning sun fell across it, the shapes within became visible. Diamonds that mirrored the weave of old village grain baskets. Spirals like the curls of water when two streams meet. Tiny lotus buds tucked into the corners, barely noticeable unless you were searching for them.

Sid had not planned these patterns exactly. They emerged from the hands of those who worked the loom—women from both sides, children tugging at spools, even the trader who insisted on "just one pass" for good luck. The cloth had begun telling its own story, one row at a time.

One afternoon, an old man from the south well approached the loom. His knees trembled with each step, but his eyes were sharp. Without asking, he leaned close to the growing fabric, tracing a trembling finger along one of the diamond patterns.

"My mother wove this," he murmured. "Not this exact cloth, but the same diamond. We used it on the canopies for weddings, before the quarrels started."

From the north well, a woman in a faded red sari lifted her head. "My grandmother used the same pattern," she said quietly. "We thought they had copied it from us."

The old man chuckled dryly. "Perhaps we copied it from each other."

A ripple of laughter passed between them—small, but real.

The cloth became a mirror. People saw in it their own histories: a line of crimson reminding one family of the bridal saris their ancestors wore; a curve of indigo recalling the border on an old festival banner. Even those who resisted the loom found themselves pausing to search for the shapes they knew.

Sid never told them it was deliberate. He had chosen patterns that lived in both sides' memory, so that each pass of the shuttle wove not only thread, but recognition.

One evening, as the sun dropped low, Sid invited the children to dip their hands in coloured water—turmeric yellow, indigo blue, hibiscus red—and press their palms onto strips of plain cotton. These handprints were then stitched into the growing cloth's border.

When the women protested that the marks were uneven, Sid only smiled. "Peace is never even. It's always shaped by the hands that dare to make it."

The trader, watching this, shook his head. "You're not just weaving cloth. You're weaving a flag."

Sid paused. "Not a flag. A memory. And a memory that belongs to both sides can't be torn so easily."

The old man from the south and the woman from the north began meeting at the loom without noticing they were doing it. They didn't speak much, but they worked side by side, their hands passing the shuttle back and forth.

One morning, the old man's shuttle slipped and landed in the woman's lap. Instead of tossing it back, she threaded it for him before handing it over. It was such a small gesture, yet the young dervish saw it and whispered to Sid, "The pattern is speaking louder than the quarrels now."

That night, under the banyan tree, Sid touched the gold thread, now almost invisible among the other colours. It no longer needed to shine alone; it had found its place in the larger design.

He realised then that peace was not about making the gold thread dominate—it was about making sure it could live alongside every other colour without losing itself.

When people see their own stories in the same cloth, they stop pulling it apart.

Chapter Fourteen — The Wedding Under the Banyan

The banyan tree had seen births, funerals, and panchayat meetings that ended in shouting. But it had not seen a wedding in nearly three decades.

The feud between the two sides of Kherapur had even split love stories apart. Young men and women from opposite wells were told to look elsewhere, to "marry within our water." Those who dared to defy the rule either left the village forever or gave up before the vows could be spoken.

One morning, as Sid was rolling up the loom cloth to keep it safe from the dust storm brewing at the horizon, the young dervish came running, grinning so wide it was almost comical.

"They've asked for it," he said breathlessly.

"For what?" Sid asked.

"The cloth. They want it for a wedding."

Sid's hands stilled on the fabric. "Whose?"

The dervish lowered his voice, as though the wind itself might be listening. "The potter's son—from the north—and the washerwoman's niece—from the south."

The request was bold, almost reckless. But the potter and the washerwoman had gone together to the elders, each side speaking on behalf of the young couple. Perhaps it was the months of weaving, the slow dissolving of suspicion, or simply fatigue from years of stubbornness—whatever the reason, the elders gave a cautious nod.

The wedding would be held in the square, under the banyan, with the cloth as the ceremonial canopy.

Preparations began at once. Women from both sides brought flowers—marigolds, jasmine, hibiscus—stringing them into garlands while keeping an eye on each other's knots. The trader offered brass lamps "for light, not for sale." Children were sent running between houses, carrying trays of sweets and clay cups of spiced buttermilk.

For the first time, the path between the two wells was crowded not with wary glances but with purposeful footsteps.

On the morning of the wedding, Sid helped raise the cloth between four bamboo poles. The sunlight filtered through it, turning the gold threads into warm streams, the indigo into deep rivers, and the crimson into fire. Beneath it, the ground felt different, as if the earth itself had decided to be softer for the day.

The bride stepped forward first, her veil a sheer cream that let the light kiss her hair. The groom followed, adjusting the hem of his kurta nervously. When they stood together under the cloth, a hush fell—not from disapproval, but from awe.

The priest began the rites, but it was the cloth that drew everyone's gaze. Every colour, every pattern, every child's handprint seemed to speak at once: *This belongs to all of you.*

The moment came when the couple circled the sacred fire. On the second round, a gust of wind lifted the edge of the cloth, and instinctively, a woman from the north and a man from the south reached up to steady it—holding the same corner, their hands brushing for the first time in years. Neither pulled away.

When the final blessing was spoken and the crowd broke into applause, Sid looked around. People from both sides were laughing, eating, and—most telling of all—sharing the same plates of sweets without a second thought.

The young dervish leaned against the banyan and said, "Do you think it will last?"

Sid's gaze drifted to the cloth above the couple. "If the pattern holds, so will they."

That night, the cloth was not taken down. It remained over the banyan, swaying gently, as if keeping watch over the square it had helped to unite.

Peace takes root when love is celebrated openly, not hidden away.

Chapter Fifteen – The Storm That Tested the Loom

Three nights after the wedding, the air in Kherapur changed. It was not the gentle coolness that came before rain, nor the dry heat that had baked the village for months. This was different—dense, restless, charged.

Sid felt it first in his fingertips while spinning thread by the lantern. The gold filament seemed to hum in his hands, as though warning him of what was coming. By dawn, the banyan leaves were turned upside down, flashing their pale undersides to the sky, a sign every farmer knew.

By mid-morning, a wall of black clouds had gathered beyond the dunes. The wind sharpened, whistling through the narrow lanes between houses, rattling clay pots and slamming half-closed shutters. Chickens scattered, goats pressed against courtyard walls, and children ran to their mothers.

The loom cloth, still stretched proudly under the banyan from the wedding, began to twist and snap in the wind like a living thing. Each tug from the gust threatened to tear it from the bamboo poles.

Sid and the young dervish rushed to the square, only to find two groups already forming—one from the north well, one from the south. They stood watching, hesitant, as if unsure whether saving the cloth together would cross some unspoken boundary.

The old man from the south stepped forward first. "It will be gone in minutes," he said. "And with it, all we've done."

The woman in the red sari from the north crossed her arms. "Then help me tie it down."

Ropes were brought. Men clambered up the poles, gripping them as the wind shoved hard. Women held the bamboo steady, their saris snapping like banners. The young dervish darted between them with extra knots, shouting instructions over the roar.

At one point, a vicious gust ripped the cloth free from one corner. It flapped wildly, and for a terrifying second, it looked as if it might lift into the storm. But the potter's son lunged and caught it—only to find the washerwoman's niece gripping the other edge. Together, they pulled it down, pinning it against the banyan trunk until others could help secure it.

Rain came then—not in soft sheets, but in furious spears. It struck the cloth, making the gold and indigo run with water. But instead of sagging, the threads seemed to swell, holding tighter, as if the storm had woven itself into their strength.

When the worst of the wind had passed, the villagers stepped back, drenched and panting. The cloth was still there—soaked, heavy, but unbroken.

Sid walked to the centre, placing his palm on the wet fabric. "A thing made together," he said softly, "can only be destroyed together. And today, you chose not to."

The old man smiled for the first time in years. "We didn't just save the cloth. We saved the pattern."

That night, even as thunder still rumbled in the distance, the banyan square felt different. The air carried not just the scent of wet earth, but the quieter fragrance of trust beginning to dry in the sun.

Unity is tested not in calm, but in storms—and each shared trial makes the weave tighter.

DSN

Chapter Sixteen – The Market of Many Tongues

The storm rinsed Kherapur clean, but the village learned quickly that clear skies invite other kinds of weather.

On the first dry Friday after the winds, the weekly bazaar assembled on the hard-packed plain beyond the south well. Traders arrived from three directions: from the salt flats with sacks of rock salt and rumours; from the canal settlements with onions, chillies, and brassware; and from the hill tracts with baskets of herbs and stories that smelled of pine.

Kherapur had not hosted a true market in years. Suspicion is a bad merchant; it makes every bargain feel like a theft.

But news of the wedding under the banyan—and of a storm that failed to tear down a cloth—had travelled ahead of the caravans. Curiosity came with coin purses tied tightly, ready to be persuaded.

Sid and the young dervish reached the field at dawn with the two women from his village and the caravan boy. They carried three bundles: lengths of the new communal cloth to sell; a smaller square of the old Weaver's Shawl to display (not for sale); and the travelling loom, folded like a peaceful animal, ready to be opened if words failed.

The square filled with stalls that grew out of the earth as if planted: a line of earthen pots stacked like moons; a spice seller whose table looked like a painted map; a man with cheap glass bracelets that flashed like shallow water.

Children ran messages, goats argued with their ropes, and the first real scent of frying snacks in months floated across the dust.

"Markets have two languages," the trader from Kherapur muttered beside Sid, tightening his turban. "Numbers and noise. We must learn both."

***

Before the sun reached the middle of the sky, a buyer arrived with city polish in his voice. He wore a pale kurta, soft-soled shoes, and a moustache trained to look reliable.

"I hear you've made a cloth that can end quarrels," he said, smiling. "I'll take the lot."

Sid shook his head gently. "We're selling cloth, not claims."

"Very good," the buyer said smoothly, "then I'll take the cloth, for very good money."

He named a number that made the dervish blink. Two men from the north well, overhearing, nodded eagerly. Two from the south frowned, suspecting a trap. The women at the stall said nothing, watching Sid.

"Buy one length first," Sid said. "Wrap it around your bargaining table. If the day's talk grows softer, come back for more."

The buyer laughed. "You want to test me with my own customers?"

"I want you to test the cloth with your own hands," Sid replied. "Peace that is bought is rarely worn."

The buyer wavered. The number he had named had been meant to stun; these people were replying with practice. In the end, greed chose caution's clothes. He bought a single length and promised to return if the market smiled at him.

When he had gone, the old man from the south well exhaled. "You sent away more money than we've seen in a season."

Sid met his gaze. "We did not send it away. We asked it to return with good company."

***

Near noon, a woman with kohl-dark eyes and a tongue quick as a drumbeat set up three stools near the loom. She sold nothing visible. Her sign—a scrap of cloth inked with slanted letters—read: *News and Necessary Truths*.

People came and paid small coins to hear what she had gathered along the road: wages rising in the canal town; a new tax on salt; the headman of a nearby village seen at night with a bundle that clinked like secrets. She wove facts and guesses until they sounded the same.

When her eyes fell on the cloth at Sid's stall, she smiled like a cat that had remembered a door. "They say," she began, to no one in particular and therefore to everyone, "that Kherapur's two wells mix their waters now. They say a single cloth holds both their pride. They say it cannot be torn."

Murmurs rose. The dervish stiffened; the women's hands paused over their scales.

Sid walked to the three stools and paid her one coin. "Tell me a necessary truth," he said, loud enough for those pretending not to listen.

She tilted her head, amused. "The second buyer offers more than the first."

"That is a rumour," Sid said.

"It will be true if you let it," she countered.

"Another necessary truth then."

She studied him. "Peace attracts envy. Envy brings a knife. The knife doesn't always look like a knife."

Sid nodded. "And your price for that wisdom?"

"Let me sit under your cloth for one hour," she said. "People trust me more when I'm seen with trustworthy things."

Sid laughed, surprised at his own relief. "Bring your stools. But hear this: under our cloth, rumours that draw blood become mended into stories that teach. If you sit there, you accept that rule."

She tapped her coin against her teeth, considering. "Agreed," she said, and moved her small theatre beneath the shade of the woven square. Her voice, when it resumed, lost a little of its bite and found a little more of its music.

***

By midafternoon, the sun had browned faces and loosened purses. A second buyer arrived—broader shoulders, fewer words, a ledger tucked under his arm like a contract that already knew its signature.

"I don't pay for sweet talk," he said, flipping open the ledger. "I pay for thread count, dye fastness, and whether my customers return with compliments instead of complaints. Your cloth looks strong. I'll take twenty lengths if the price is honest."

This time, the south well men lit up, and the north well men grew careful—each side guarding what it had already given.

"Ten lengths," Sid said, "and you sit with us while we weave one more row. If your fingers itch to help, you'll know why the price holds."

The buyer stared at him. "You want me to work for my purchase?"

"I want you to meet the thread," Sid said. "It is shy with strangers who use only ledgers."

He surprised them by agreeing. When the loom was opened, the buyer reached with blunt, practiced hands, and though he fumbled at first, his grip gentled by the third pass. When the row was done, he nodded once, the way a man nods to a tool that doesn't splinter under pressure.

"Ten lengths," he said. "And if they sell without return, we talk of thirty."

The number was lower than the first buyer's offer had been, but the ground under it felt solid. The village chose the smaller hill that stood rather than the glittering river that might have been a mirage.

***

As coins changed hands and cloth disappeared into sacks bound for far towns, a third visitor came—a woman in a pale blue sari with edges sharp as her gaze. She introduced herself as the agent of a mill. Her words were smooth and practical, like oiled gears.

"You have built a story," she said to Sid. "We can give it a factory. We will take your patterns, colours, motifs—and this whole 'two-wells' myth—and print tens of thousands. Your village will earn royalties. No more weaving in the heat. No more sore backs. Peace, at scale."

The young dervish's eyes went wide. The caravan boy swallowed. Even the two women from Sid's village exchanged a glance. The old man's mouth set into a thin line.

Sid asked the agent for a moment and gathered his people into a small circle. "Speak," he said.

The woman weaver said, "Royalties could repair roofs and buy goats."

The old man said, "A pattern printed is a pattern that forgets the hands that made it."

The dervish said, "But think of how many quarrels it could soften."

The caravan boy said nothing; he looked at the loom and chewed his lip.

Sid listened. He thought of Viren's gold thread—how it frayed if pulled too fast. He saw the Bodhi leaf in his mind—how stillness had taught him to stay where he was when everything tried to move him. He heard the boatman: *Don't knot it too tight.* He remembered the mountain weaver: *Weave with them, not for them.*

He returned to the agent. "We'll sell cloth by our hands, not our story by the thousand. If your mill wishes to buy lengths we have woven, we can discuss fair numbers. But if you wish to print our pattern without our pace, the price is not money—it is the muscle that keeps peace alive. That, we will not sell."

The agent's face did not change, but her eyes shuttered a fraction. "Sentiment is expensive," she said.

"Cheaper than forgetting," Sid replied.

She left without purchasing. The rumour seller watched her go and murmured, "Knives sometimes come wrapped in satin."

"And sometimes satin learns to be thread," Sid said. "If it returns to us as cloth, we'll treat it kindly."

***

Late in the day, the market slowed to its warm, tired chatter. A group of labourers from a canal project approached the stall with callused hands and shoulders that sagged with the day's weight. They stared at the weaving lengths as if looking at water they could not yet drink.

"Sit," Sid said, before they asked. "One row each."

They protested, for they had dirty hands, rough palms, and no time, but the women from Kherapur stopped them with pots of water and handed them cloths to wipe with. The dervish guided their fingers; the caravan boy oiled the shuttle track. The labourers wove like men who thought they were unworthy and discovered they were not.

When they rose to leave, one of them placed a bundle of onions on the stall, more than the cost of a small length. "For the cloth," he said.

"For the row you made," Sid corrected, and split the onions, sending some to the north and some to the south without counting.

The old man watched this and sighed. "Every time we pass the shuttle, it seems lighter."

"Because it is shared," the woman weaver said. "Two hands lift a weight the mind insists is one."

***

As the sun dropped, lamps were lit, coins were counted, and day's dust rose in a last, lazy cloud. The first buyer returned, moustache untidy, smile less certain.

"How did your bargaining table fare?" Sid asked.

The man tugged his collar. "People argued less. It cost me more concessions than I like. But I sold more. I'll take five lengths."

They wrapped his purchase without triumph, only with the quiet satisfaction of a bargain that had learned its maths.

The rumour seller rose from her stools under the cloth. “A necessary truth for the road,” she told Sid. “Today, your village learned to speak three languages—numbers, noise, and notice.”

“Notice?” the dervish asked.

She tipped her head at the scene: the labourers’ onions split fairly; the two wells’ women counting coins together; the children asleep under the stall, cheeks dusted with turmeric and sugar. “You noticed what had to be seen before it could be sold.”

She packed her stools and, after a pause, tucked one coloured thread into her bag. “For my sign,” she said. “It needs a border.”

***

When the field emptied, the travellers and villagers sat in a rough circle, legs extended, backs slack with honest fatigue. They counted coins into three piles: one for the Kherapur loom fund, one for the two sheds to repair frames, and one smaller pile for thread and dye.

The agent’s offer returned like a moth around a lamp. No one raised it again, but everyone felt its soft-walled cage. Sid finally spoke.

“Peace must be portable, but not printable,” he said. “We carry it by hand, not by machine. If we grow too fast, we will snap where we were meant to bend.”

The old man nodded. The women murmured agreement. The dervish yawned in the last light and said, “Tomorrow, we weave slower.”

"Tomorrow, we weave as fast as trust," Sid corrected. "No slower, no faster."

They laughed—quiet, contented, the laughter of a market that had not been cheated. The moon rose, and the cloth folded on the cart seemed to glow from within, storing the day's voices like a ledger no one could falsify.

Grow at the speed of trust; sell at the price of your practice.

III

Chapter Seventeen – The Letter from the Hills

The market's coins still clinked faintly in the minds of Kherapur's people when a runner arrived at dawn.

He was barefoot, dusty up to his knees, carrying no pack, only a cloth tube strapped across his back. His breath came sharp but steady, the rhythm of someone who had crossed more than one valley in a single night.

He found Sid in the shed where the loom slept. The young dervish was oiling the shuttle track; the women were sorting onion skins for dye; the old man was still rubbing the ache from his knees after the market.

The runner touched his forehead, then unrolled a length of handwoven hemp. Inside, wrapped with care, was a folded letter bound with a thin strand of gold thread—the same thread Viren had given Sid months ago in the high passes.

The wax seal was a pressed Bodhi leaf.

***

Sid broke the seal slowly, as if each crack might wake the asleep. The script was lean, the hand of a man who wasted neither ink nor breath.

Sid,

The cloth you began has reached the hills before the monsoon did.

I have seen two lengths in the hands of traders who spoke your name with the care one gives to water in a drought.

There is a valley beyond my own where the people drink from a single spring but quarrel over the paths to reach it.

They will listen to you because you are not from among them.

They will argue with you because you carry something they think they deserve without asking.

Bring the cloth. Bring the loom. Bring the story.

I will meet you where the cedar roots drink from the stone.

Come before the snows.

Viren

The room was quiet after Sid read it aloud. The old man's eyes narrowed—not with suspicion, but with the habit of weighing cost against gain. The young dervish smiled faintly, as if he had been waiting for the road to call again. The women kept sorting onion skins, but their fingers slowed.

***

"Another village," the old man said. "Another fight that isn't ours."

"Peace doesn't belong," the dervish replied. "It visits."

"Visits cost food," the old man countered. "And the loom is just beginning to belong here."

The women finally spoke. "If the cloth can cross hills, it can return with more than coins. It can return with dye we have not seen, with patterns our children will remember."

Sid listened, feeling the weight of Viren's gold thread in his palm. The temptation was to see the road as a straight line—leave now, return later. But threads that pull too quickly fray.

***

That evening, they gathered under the banyan where the wedding cloth had first been shown. The north well and south well sent their elders; and the rumour seller appeared uninvited, her stools folded under her arm.

When Sid read the letter again, a low hum went through the crowd. Some saw the hills as an opportunity; others saw them as a thief waiting to take away what little had been stitched here.

One man from the north well spoke bluntly: "If you leave, the loom will stall. And without the loom, the peace between wells will dry like an untended rope."

A woman from the south well answered, "If he does not leave, the cloth will never learn new languages. It will speak only Kherapur's tongue, and soon even that will grow stale."

The rumour seller stood on her stools. "Necessary truth," she said. "Peace is a guest that grows restless if kept too long in one house."

She stepped down without further comment, leaving the sentence to weave itself through their minds.

***

In the end, Sid stood. "The cloth is not mine, nor is it only Kherapur's. It belongs to every hand that lifts the shuttle, here or beyond the hills. I will go. But I will not take the whole loom."

He proposed to leave the main frame in Kherapur, with the women as its keepers and the old man as its steward. He would carry only the travelling loom—the peaceful animal that folded down to fit on a cart.

"If quarrels rise while I am gone," he said, "feed them through the loom until they come out as cloth. When I return, we will join your weavings with mine."

The old man frowned but nodded. "Threads cut in half can be knotted again, if they are kept clean."

***

The days that followed were full of quiet industry. The women dyed three lengths in deep indigo and tied them with white thread for Sid to carry. The dervish prepared the loom's smaller frame and checked each peg and shuttle for cracks. The old man carved a new beam to replace the worn one, muttering about how travellers forget that wood needs tending.

The caravan boy, who had not spoken much since the market, came to Sid at dusk. "Take me," he said simply.

Sid studied him. "Why?"

"Because I've carried cloth," the boy said, "but I've never carried a story while it was still being made."

Sid smiled. "Then you will carry both."

***

On the last night, Sid walked alone to the ridge above the village. Below, the two wells glimmered in moonlight, their waters indistinguishable from this height. Somewhere in the dark, the loom's wood creaked as if it knew it would be working without him for a while.

He took out Viren's gold thread and wound it once around his wrist, then once around the handle of the travelling loom. The knot was simple, loose enough to undo, but enough to remind him: connection is not possession.

From the hills, the wind carried the faint scent of cedar.

To carry peace, you must be willing to leave it behind in safe hands.

DSN

Chapter Eighteen – The Valley of One Spring

The journey to the hills took eight days.

They travelled at dawn and rested when the sun struck like a hammer. The road was a thread between fields of millet and mustard, then into rockier slopes where the air thinned and the smell of cedar replaced that of wet soil.

The caravan boy learned quickly—how to tighten the cloth bundles so they rode evenly, how to keep the travelling loom's pegs from working loose, and how to read the shadow of a vulture as a sign of where goats might graze.

On the ninth morning, they crossed a ridge and saw the valley. From above, it looked peaceful: terraced fields like steps down into green, the glimmer of water catching the sun in the centre. But Viren had warned them—the beauty was the mask.

***

At the heart of the valley, a single spring gushed from a cleft in the rock, its water pooling into a deep, stone-lined basin before spilling into channels that fed the fields. From this source, two wide paths wound away—one east, one west.

Each path led to a settlement, and each settlement claimed the spring as its own. The east side had painted its houses in pale ochres and blues, and their balconies draped with drying corn. The west side's houses were plain stone, but each doorway was marked with a strip of dyed cloth, as if colour itself was a statement.

The quarrel was not over the water, because both the sides drank freely. The quarrel was over *who poured first*. For years, the elders had met at the spring at dawn, taking turns to draw the first bucket. But lately, the turns had been broken.

***

When Sid, the dervish, and the boy entered the east settlement, they were met with polite caution. The headwoman, a tall figure in a saffron shawl, offered them tea but asked twice whether their cloth was for trade or for gift. Sid answered, "Neither. It is for weaving peace."

She smiled tightly. "Peace is woven from power here, stranger. And power drinks first."

Across the valley, the west settlement was less polite. A cluster of men met them at the edge, one carrying a staff carved with the image of the spring. The leader was a man with hair like silver threads. He eyed the travelling loom strapped to the donkey. "If you've come to weave for them," he said, nodding toward the east, "we have no need for your cloth."

"I have come to weave *with* you," Sid replied. "With both."

The silver-haired man snorted. "The last person who said that went home with an empty pot."

***

That evening, as they camped midway between the two paths, a shadow fell across the fire. Viren emerged from the darkness, his walking stick wrapped in strips of cedar bark. He looked older, but his eyes still held the same deep calm.

"You've seen the paths," he said after greetings were exchanged. "Now you must see the pride. The water is pure, but it flows through veins of stone. And stone remembers grudges longer than rivers remember floods."

Sid asked, "And the loom?"

Viren smiled faintly. "It will not weave unless both bring their thread. And neither will bring theirs unless they believe the cloth will hang where both can see it."

***

The next morning, Viren called for the elders of both settlements to meet at the spring. They arrived stiff-backed, eyes darting to see who stood closer to the water. Sid placed the travelling loom on the flat stone beside the basin.

"This loom has stood in desert dust," he told them, "and in the square of a village that had two wells but one thirst. It will stand here, by your spring, for three days. Anyone may bring thread. Anyone may lift the shuttle. But the cloth will not leave this stone until both your dyes touch it."

From the east, the headwoman frowned. "And if we refuse?"

"Then the loom will leave," Sid said simply, "and you will still have the same quarrel, only with one more thing to envy—the peace you could not weave."

***

No one moved the first day. The loom sat untouched under the cedar shade, its pegs catching the light. Sid and Viren did not press; they sat nearby, mending their own travel cloths, letting the quiet weigh on the valley.

On the second day, a boy from the west settlement wandered to the loom, trailing a strip of undyed wool. He placed it in the shuttle and made two hesitant passes. From the east, a girl about his age arrived with a length of saffron-dyed cotton. She did not speak to him, but she placed her thread next to his.

By evening, a small square of cloth had begun to form.

***

On the third morning, the headwoman from the east arrived with a bundle of pale blue silk. The silver-haired man from the west came with thick wool dyed in deep crimson. They stood on opposite sides of the loom, each waiting for the other to step forward.

Finally, Viren said, "The spring gives to all without asking who drinks first. Will you let cloth be more stubborn than water?"

The headwoman placed her silk in the shuttle. The silver-haired man guided it through, then added his wool. The pattern that emerged was unlike either side's work—a mingling of softness and strength, heat and cool.

***

When the three days were over, the finished cloth was hung on the rock face above the spring. The water spilled beneath it, catching its colours in the ripples. People came from both sides to see it, and while no one declared the quarrel ended, they drew water without shouting that morning.

Sid knew it was only the first thread in a larger weaving. But as the cedar wind moved the cloth gently over the spring, he thought of Kherapur and how even the tightest knots loosen if the loom keeps moving.

Peace cannot be owned. It must be left where all can see it, touch it, and claim it together.

DSN

Chapter Nineteen – The Thread That Came Loose

Peace is shy in daylight and bolder by lamplight. For three evenings after the cloth was hung above the spring, people came at dusk to sit on the flat rocks and let the water's mutter fold over their talk.

The headwoman from the east and the silver-haired elder from the west kept a cautious truce, arriving at opposite hours and leaving without ceremony.

Children discovered that echoes were kinder if you laughed softly. The cloth lifted and settled in the cedar breeze, its colours borrowing the cool from the water.

On the fourth morning, a cry went up from the path.

"Cut!"

Sid and Viren reached the spring to find a jagged slit running through the cloth's lower quarter, like a wound that had not decided whether to close or speak. Threads dangled—blue silk, crimson wool, saffron cotton—each one abruptly ending where a blade had argued with patience.

The valley gathered fast. Accusations arrived before breath.

"They could not stand to see our dye higher," someone from the west spat.

"You hated the silk from the start," an east woman snapped.

The headwoman's jaw hardened; the silver-haired elder's hands shook on his staff. The spring kept flowing with its steady, indifferent mercy.

Sid did not speak. He reached up, touched the torn edge, and brought his fingers away slow, as if greeting the damage in the way you greet a frightened animal.

"Who?" a boy demanded, eyes wide with the awful thrill of a mystery.

"Not 'who' yet," Sid said. "First comes 'how', so we learn what must be mended."

Viren's eyes moved over the cut. "Not a clean knife. A hurried one. Dull. And pulled downward, by a hand that shook."

Murmurs shifted. A clean sabotage would have been pride; this felt like panic.

"Take it down?" the silver-haired man asked, voice tight.

"No," Sid said. "If a wound is honest, we dress it where it was made."

He unrolled the travelling kit: bone needles, spare thread, a small square of undyed cotton, and the last of Viren's gold. His hands arranged tools the way a priest lays out lamps. Then he sat on the rock ledge, level with the tear, and waited.

"Bring me the person who holds the fear that used this blade," he said quietly. "If not, bring me silence, and we will sew with that."

Silence came first. Then, from the west path, a shuffle. A boy—perhaps twelve—pushed through the ring of legs, cheeks open with shame.

Behind him hovered a man with a moustache like two small scythes; his eyes flickered away from the cloth.

The boy's words tumbled. "I ... my uncle ... he said the silk claimed too much water ... he said it would hang like their flag forever ... he gave me the knife ... and said to cut just the bottom so it falls ... only a little ... so it can be rehung lower ..."

The uncle hissed, "Foolish child," and tried to seize his shoulder, but the crowd's weight shifted, closing him out. The boy stood alone with his mistake.

Sid did not ask why the uncle had not carried his own blade. Cowardice is boring when exposed to air. He patted the rock beside him.

"Sit."

The boy sat, rigid as a pulled thread. His breathing came in small, frightened stitches.

Sid threaded a needle, first with plain cotton. He placed it in the boy's palm.

"You cut," he said softly. "You will mend."

The boy stared. "I don't know how."

"Good," Sid said. "Then your hands will listen."

He guided the first pass through both torn edges, wide and visible, not hidden. Each stitch was a confession that made the cloth more honest. People flinched at the audacity of showing the repair. The headwoman took a breath as if to object. Viren lifted a finger—not to silence her, but to ask her to wait for the pattern to speak.

They stitched the tear closed with the plain cotton—slow, uneven, true. The boy's hands shook less by the fourth pass. "It's ugly," he whispered.

"It's a scar," Sid said. "Scars teach longer than skin."

When the edges held, Sid pulled out the gold. He tied it to the boy's cotton with a knot so small you could miss it unless you were the one making it.

"Now," he said, "we honour the damage."

He ran the gold thread over the plain repair in a ladder, then in a small crossing pattern that caught light whenever the breeze lifted the cloth. The tear did not disappear; it transformed. It became a seam that shone.

"What is this?" the silver-haired elder asked, voice roughened by something like relief.

"Visible mending," Viren answered. "We do not hide what happened. We bind it so strongly that future quarrels must account for its strength."

From the east, a woman exhaled. "Our grandmothers used to echo broken pottery with gold in the seams."

"Our grandfathers patched leather with bright thread to find the tear again in story," a man from the west added, surprised by his own memory.

The uncle tried to step backward into anonymity. The headwoman's voice, cool and even, stopped him.

"Not yet."

Sid looked at him, but not unkindly. "You owe the spring a repair."

The man's mouth twisted. "I owe the spring?"

"You used it as a stage," Sid said. "Now use it as a classroom."

He handed the man the needle. The uncle's fingers—strong from harvests, clumsy with shame—followed the boy's stitches, crossing where the gold had begun, completing a pattern he had tried to unmake. When he knotted off, he did not meet anyone's eyes.

Sid stood and faced both settlements.

"In Kherapur," he said, "we learned that mixed water rinses cloth cleaner than either well alone. In this valley, you will learn that mixed hands mend stronger than single pride."

He turned to the headwoman and the elder. "Make it a rule: whoever cuts must mend; whoever mends must teach; and whoever taught must hang the cloth back where all can see."

The headwoman considered. "And when no one admits the cut?"

"Then the elder of the opposite side mends the tear," Sid said. "And the guilt of the hidden hand will grow louder than our quiet."

The elder's mouth twitched—half smile, half concession. "A fair cruelty," he said.

They rehung the cloth. The gold ladder glimmered like a small, stubborn promise. Children pointed, already repeating the story wrong and therefore exactly right for its survival.

At dusk, the boy lingered by the spring. The uncle stood apart, chastened into silence. Sid touched the repaired seam.

"What will they say of me?" the boy asked, eyes worried by a future he could not measure.

"That you learned," Sid said. "That your hands helped where your fear had harmed. And some will forget even that, which is also a kind of peace."

He handed the boy the empty spool that had held the gold. "Keep this. When your hands itch to cut, wind them around it first."

The boy nodded and left with the careful dignity of someone carrying a cup without water but with purpose.

When the crowd thinned, the headwoman approached the silver-haired elder. "Tomorrow, you draw first," she said.

He shook his head. "No. Tomorrow, we pour together."

And in the morning, they did. Two buckets tilted into one basin until their waters found the same level without argument.

Viren looked at the seam, then at Sid. "Once mended, the tear becomes the strongest line."

Sid smiled, tired and light. "And the most remembered."

The spring kept talking to stone, patient as ever. Above it, the cloth breathed with the valley's wind—scarred, brighter, and better instructed.

Do not hide the tear; mend it where all can see—so the seam teaches what pride forgets.

DSN

Chapter Twenty – The Pilgrim's Gift

The valley woke to a sound it did not recognize—a low, clear tone that seemed to come from the stone itself, as if the mountain had spoken and then decided to let the note linger.

Sid opened his eyes to dawn filing the pine needles with silver. The travelling loom slept under its cloth, the boy curled against the beam, the young dervish already sitting cross-legged, listening.

The tone came again: a soft circle of sound that widened without shouting, a ripple over still water. They followed it to the spring.

A woman stood there—barefoot, dust to her shins, hair bound with a strip of saffron cloth gone pale with sun. She was neither young nor old, the sort of age that has practiced being both.

In her hands she held a small copper bowl, its lip bright where it had met many mornings. Along one side, a fine seam of gold stitched a hairline crack, catching the light the way a river catches sky.

She struck the bowl once with a thin cedar stick. The note rose again, walked the rocks, and sat down among the people gathering from both paths.

"Pilgrim," Viren said softly, and the word felt correct in the mouth.

She inclined her head with the ease of someone who bowed to roads as often as to gods. "I ask the valley's permission to drink," she said, voice calm as a well that knows its depth.

"Permission?" the silver-haired elder said, startled into courtesy. "This spring belongs to all."

"Then let your belonging start with a stranger," she replied.

The headwoman stepped forward. "Please drink."

The pilgrim dipped the bowl. The water slid against the gold seam, hesitated as if reading it, then rested. She raised the bowl, did not drink, and instead turned to the east path. "You first," she said to a child who had come running with a copper cup dented into the shape of hunger.

The boy looked to his mother. The mother looked to the headwoman. The headwoman glanced at the elder. Agreement passed like a quiet coin. The child drank, blinked at his good luck, and ran back to whatever game the morning had promised him.

Only then did the pilgrim drink. The note of the bowl seemed to have taught her throat how.

"Who repairs a bowl with gold?" someone from the west murmured, half-amused, half-wary. "Who wastes brightness on cracks?"

"Those who refuse to waste a crack," the pilgrim said, hearing without being told. "This seam remembers every hand that has carried this water. It asks for good company."

She set the bowl on the rock beside the cloth that hung above the spring, its gold ladder-seam glinting in slow conversation with the bowl's repair.

Two visible mendings nodded to each other like relatives who had only just learned the family story.

Sid felt the meeting of those glints in his chest—the bowl's gold, the cloth's gold, the morning's thin gold spread over water. It made a quiet triad that did not ask to be noticed and was stronger for being together.

"Where do you carry your feet?" the dervish asked, smiling.

"Where thirst points," the pilgrim said. "I walk the old routes, the ones even maps forget, carrying a rule for shared water."

"A rule?" the elder asked, suspicious but tempted.

"The Pilgrim's Rule," she said, as if repeating a joke that had grown true from frequent telling. "At any shared source, the first water each dawn belongs to the one who slept farthest from it."

Murmurs rose like birds. The headwoman arched an eyebrow. "And if no one slept farther than we did?"

"Then the first water goes to the quietest throat," the pilgrim said, not missing a beat. "You can hear it when you listen. It is never the throat at the front."

Viren's mouth held a ghost of a smile. "You are a poor seller of cups."

"I do not sell," the pilgrim said. "I carry reminders."

She lifted the bowl and offered it—not to the headwoman *or* the elder, but to Sid. "Hold this while I speak."

He did. The copper hummed against his palm, a memory of the struck note still walking its circle.

"I have heard of your cloth," she went on, looking from one path to the other. "And of the gold that made a wound honest. I bring a companion for it, if the valley will keep the rule by which it lives."

"What rule?" the elder pressed, though his eyes had already softened in the way a man's eyes soften when he recognizes a good tool.

"The bowl drinks only if a stranger drinks first," she said. "The Stranger's Cup." She tapped the gold seam with the cedar stick. "This cup remembers hands. It wants new ones daily."

Silence considered this. Even the spring seemed to pause.

The headwoman broke the stillness with a small smile. "We have argued for years over who drinks first. Perhaps the spring has grown bored with us. Let it meet other mouths."

A boy from the west—older than the first, proud in the way boys are when they carry things high—raised his hand. "If no stranger comes?"

"Then you make one," the pilgrim said. "You choose the far edge of yourself—someone you have not listened to for too long. Give them the bowl. Ask them what the water tasted like, and believe their answer."

A slow laugh rippled, a laugh that had folded its arms long ago and now remembered how to uncross them.

"Will you leave the bowl?" the elder asked, practical as a harvest.

"If the valley takes the rule," she replied. "The bowl stays where rules stay—in habit, not in shrines."

Sid held the copper, turning it once. The gold seam caught a sliver of sun and threw it onto the water, where it broke into many small coins of light.

He thought of Kherapur's shared basin, the day two buckets tilted together. He thought of the boy who had cut the cloth and then mended it where all could see. He thought of the market woman who changed her tone beneath the loom. These were not miracles. They were remembered gestures.

"We will keep it," the headwoman said, "if you will teach us how to do the keeping."

The pilgrim nodded. "Three dawns. Three lessons."

DSN

Chapter Twenty-One – The Three Dawns

They met before the sun lifted the cedar shadows from the rock. The pilgrim struck the bowl lightly; the note walked across their shoulders and told their spines to grow quiet. People from both paths stood in a half-circle, some clutching cups, some clutching habits.

"The first water," the pilgrim said, "belongs to the breath that has travelled farthest to reach here."

She pointed to a man who had arrived in the night carrying a bundle of tools, eyes tired as heel-worn sandals. "Road-mender," she said. "Please drink."

He bowed, surprised at being seen without asking to be. He drank. He did not give a speech. He only said, "Sweet," and the valley believed him.

"Now," the pilgrim went on, "before anyone else drinks, we listen to three breaths. The spring's. Your own. Your neighbour's." She waited while they obeyed. The water's breath was a mutter. Their own were uneven, then less so. Their neighbour's were too fast, then found the pace of hearing.

"Pour," she said, and they did.

That day, quarrels arrived late and left early. It was not peace, but it was practice.

***

On the second day, again came the note and the half circle of bodies learning to bend toward a centre without bowing to each other. The pilgrim lifted the bowl.

"Second lesson. The bowl drinks names. Not titles. Not debts."

She gave it to a woman who had never stood at the front of any line. "Say your name to the water," the pilgrim said.

The woman whispered it. The water kept it gently and gave it back as a reflection. She drank, and when she lowered the bowl, the line had re-ordered itself without anyone insisting, as if names had rearranged gravity.

"Now a name from the other path," the pilgrim said. A young man spoke his, voice brittle with old arguments. The bowl did not flinch. He drank. Some shoulders relaxed.

They poured. They counted breaths without counting coins. The spring did not chide or favour. It rolled itself thin over their stubbornness and wore it smooth in places.

***

On the third morning, a bank of cloud held the light hostage a little longer. The pilgrim struck the bowl only once, then set the cedar stick aside.

"Final lesson," she said. "Some mornings, the bowl must remain empty until you have made a place for it."

A puzzled murmur moved through the half circle.

"Who came early and swept this rock?" she asked.

A child raised a hand, uncertain. A smear of damp grit marked his ankle where he had slipped and kept his feet anyway.

"Then the first water belongs to the one who made room for it," the pilgrim said, and the child's grin became a small sun the clouds could not hold.

After he drank, she did something that startled even Sid: she tipped the bowl gently, letting a thin thread of water slide back into the spring.

Gasps, quickly hushed.

"The bowl must learn to return," she said. "Otherwise, it becomes persuasion, not companion."

She handed the bowl to the silver-haired elder. "Tomorrow, you keep it. The next day, she keeps it," she added, tipping her chin toward the headwoman. "Then pass it to hands that have not been trusted. You will know them."

"And you?" the headwoman asked. "Where will you go?"

"Where thirst points," the pilgrim said again, and smiled with a kind of tired radiance that travellers wear when they are both ready to sit and not allowed to.

She turned to Sid. "You carry a cloth that remembers many lessons. Add this: the first sip belongs to the farthest mouth. If you forget, strike the bowl and listen to your stubbornness soften."

Sid bowed. "Stay one more day."

"I have already stayed one more day," she said, and her kindness made refusal taste less like no and more like a completed row.

She walked without hurry to the edge of the cedar shade, then farther, becoming a small moving seam between two fields of green and a sky that was still deciding how to begin. When she was a thread's width, the pilgrim turned and lifted her bowl—empty now, gold seam catching one last note of light. Then she tucked it under her arm and was part of the road again.

Except the bowl was on the rock.

Sid blinked. So did Viren. So did the headwoman, then laughed at her own slow seeing.

The pilgrim had left the bowl behind and carried only the seam in her pace.

***

They argued a little over where to set the bowl, which pleased the pilgrim's rule—it likes a short argument before a long habit. Finally, they chose a shallow niche in the rock where the spring rose. The bowl rested there, dry between uses, gold seam facing outward like a warning against quiet damage and a welcome to loud repair.

The first stranger who came after the pilgrim was a shepherd with dust the colour of old almonds on his calves and a cough that had learned to be polite. He drank from the bowl without understanding its story, and the spring made no demand that he did. The valley did that part—someone explained, someone nodded, someone struck the cedar stick once, lightly.

Sid watched three dawns pass with the bowl kissing different mouths first. He saw something small and stubborn shift in the valley's stance—the way men planted their feet near the spring, the way women's shoulders lowered half a finger's breadth when the note walked the rock.

On the fourth morning, he stood beside the cloth and the bowl and felt them speaking to each other without needing his translation. One glinted in a ladder that honoured a wound; the other carried a seam that honoured a long journey. Between them, the spring did what it had always done—offered itself without ledger.

"You look relieved," Viren said.

"I look unemployed," Sid said, and they both smiled at the joke and the truth inside it.

Let the first water go to the farthest mouth; hospitality is the quietest beginning of peace.

DSN

Chapter Twenty-Two —
The Weaver's Silence

By the time the pilgrim's absence had settled into the valley like a chair no one sat in anymore, the loom had begun to speak in its own way.

Not in words—never in words—but in the pauses between the shuttle's passes, the way a listener can learn the meaning of a song by its rests.

Sid had moved the loom closer to the spring, under the cedar whose roots had always found the water first.

Here, the cloth's gold ladder met the morning's gold spill without anyone needing to lift it.

The villagers had stopped standing in two lines.

Instead, they leaned in an uneven crescent around the work, as if afraid they might accidentally agree on something if they stood too straight.

It was on one of these mornings that an old woman from the west path arrived, carrying a bundle wrapped in indigo cloth.

Her back was straight, but her eyes were bent inward in the way of someone who had learned to visit herself more than she visited others.

She set the bundle down beside Sid without speaking. He waited, sensing that the silence was not an absence but a bridge.

When she finally unwrapped the cloth, the smell came first—earth after rain, woodsmoke, and something like saffron that had never been near a kitchen.

Inside lay a weaving frame no bigger than two outstretched hands, its warp already strung but bare of weft.

The threads were pale as ash before a wind takes it.

"This," she said at last, voice a soft grit, "was my grandmother's. She wove during famine so that her hands would not forget the feel of food."

Sid reached for the frame, then stopped.

"You want me to finish it?"

"No," she said, and the refusal was gentle but solid.

"I want you to listen to it. It holds a pattern I cannot speak without breaking it."

***

That night, he sat by the loom's larger shadow and held the small frame in his lap.

The warp hummed under his fingers, taut with memory. It was a different hum from the pilgrim's bowl, but related—like two branches cut from the same tree decades apart.

He closed his eyes.

At first there was nothing, only the push of his own breathing.

Then he began to hear the loom the way you hear a river from far off—not as water, but as insistence.

The weft that was missing did not feel like a gap.

It felt like a question, waiting.

When he opened his eyes again, the fire was low, the moon had turned the spring into a white coin, and Viren was sitting across from him, watching.

"Well?" Viren asked.

"It's not for me to weave," Sid said.

"It's for me to keep empty."

***

The next morning, Sid did not touch the larger loom.

He set the small frame in the centre of the cedar shade, between the bowl and the cloth.

The villagers noticed immediately.

Some frowned. Some whispered.

One child asked, "Is it broken?"

"No," Sid said. "It's listening."

The headwoman tilted her head. "To what?"

"To the thread that hasn't arrived yet."

It was the elder who surprised everyone by nodding first.

"We have all been threads in waiting," he said quietly.

"We forget too quickly what that feels like."

***

By midday, no one had woven, not even the children who usually begged to throw the shuttle.

Instead, they sat in small knots, talking less than usual, and looking—really looking—at the people they usually spoke *around*.

At sunset, the small frame remained empty.

The ash-pale warp caught the dying light and turned it into a thin ladder that led nowhere.

Or perhaps to somewhere no one could name yet.

That night, Sid covered it with the indigo cloth and placed it beside the pilgrim's copper bowl.

Two objects, two rules—one for the mouth, one for the hands.

The bowl said: *The first sip belongs to the farthest mouth.*

The frame said: *Leave space for what you do not yet know how to hold.*

***

On the third day, the old woman returned. She lifted the indigo cloth, looked at the untouched frame, and nodded.

"You heard it," she said.

"I heard that it wasn't mine to finish," Sid replied.

She smiled, a small, cracked thing that looked like it had been in storage for years.

"That is the pattern."

She took the frame and walked away, not toward either path but into the cedar's deeper shade, where light went to become memory.

Not all unfinished things are waiting for your hands; some are waiting for your patience.

DSN

Chapter Twenty-Three – The Cedar Lesson

After the day of the small, empty loom, the valley moved with a quieter stride.

People did not stop weaving; they simply wove with pauses, in spaces where a row might have been. The pilgrim's bowl learned new lips each dawn, and the gold ladder on the cloth kept catching the sun like a promise that had learned to be modest.

Sid woke before the birds and sat beneath the cedar whose roots drank the spring like an old friend. The bark was ridged with years. When he pressed his palm against it, the tree did not speak, but it agreed—to what, he could not have said, only that consent moved up his arm like a slow, warm thread.

The young dervish joined him, stretching sleep from his shoulders.

"You're listening to a tree now," he said, half teasing.

"Better student than most men," Sid replied.

They smiled, and the cedar held their joke the way elders hold a child's first secret, with pride and silence.

***

Before noon, a woman arrived from the east path carrying a strip of bark and a tool that looked like a knife that had remembered gentleness. She laid the bark in her lap and began shaving it into thin curls, each one pale as a fingernail moon.

"My father taught me cedar-mending," she said without introduction. "In winter, the bark cracks. We do not stitch it shut, instead, we make a bridge."

She showed them: a sliver of bark softened in water, laid across the split, tied with fibre that would rot at the right season.

"The tree grows round the help," she said. "If we stitch tight, it strangles. If we bridge loose, it heals."

Sid thought of the valley's cloth, of the gold ladder that honoured the cut without pretending it never happened.

"Bridges, not stitches," he murmured.

The silver-haired elder had been listening from the shade. "Our quarrel used to be a tight seam," he said. "We wore it until it cut the skin."

The woman handed him the tool. "Cut less," she said simply.

He laughed, a short, surprised sound that returned to him lighter than it left.

***

For three days, they turned the cedar grove into a small school.

Children learned to soften bark in a clay bowl, to lay it across a sap-split without forcing it, to wind fibre with patience and a little song the woman taught them that sounded like rain learning to fall.

Adults watched, pretending to supervise when they were remembering how to learn.

The headwoman knelt, surprising everyone including herself, and practiced on a low branch as if confessing to it.

The elder worked slower than pride liked but faster than habit feared.

Sid carved a small sign and hung it from a twine loop on the cedar's lowest limb:

BRIDGE, DON'T STRANGLE.

The dervish raised an eyebrow. "You've become a sign-maker."

"Only because the tree refuses to write," Sid said.

***

On the fourth morning, a man arrived from a farther valley. He wore no colour but dust and had the look of someone who had given all his thoughts to a problem and received none back. He stood near the spring and did not approach the bowl.

Sid walked to him. "Drink?"

"I have come to find a rule to take home," the man said. "I have no money to pay for it."

"Rules are like water here," Sid replied. "We don't sell them, and we don't help those who won't carry them."

The man's mouth twitched with the beginning of a smile. "I will carry."

Sid led him to the cedar class. The bark-mender placed a sliver and the gentle blade in his hands. He tried to stitch; the cedar refused. He tried again; the bark split. On the third attempt, his breath slowed, his fingers softened, and the bridge lay across the wound as if it had grown there.

"What is the rule?" he asked, voice low.

"Bridge first," the woman said. "Name the split, bring something that can rot, and trust the tree to finish what you began."

The man nodded. He drank from the bowl—because strangers with empty hands drink first—and left with two lessons: one for water, one for wood.

***

That evening, at the edge of the cedar light, two songs rose from opposite paths.

One was a work chant from the east, all bright steps and quick claps.

The other was a harvest drone from the west, low and long as a hill's shadow.

They had always been sung on different nights so no one would have to hear the other. Tonight, they started at the same hour by accident, then on purpose.

For a minute, the songs argued as songs do—this rhythm or that, this speed or slower.

Sid lifted the cedar stick and tapped the pilgrim's bowl once. The note found a common space between the chants, a pocket of air where both could live without stepping on each other's toes. The singers paused, listened, and without saying a word, shifted half a beat.

The two songs became one braid—still distinct strands, now sharing a spine.

Viren, who had been quiet all day, cleared his throat. "We should ask the cedar to charge fees," he said.

"It already does," Sid replied. "We pay in listening."

***

That night, by firelight and cedar resin's sweet smoke, Sid wrote a letter on rough hemp for the old man and the women who kept Kherapur's loom.

The hills have a spring and two songs that learned to share a beat.

We taught their hands to bridge and not strangle.

A pilgrim left us a bowl that listens.

If quarrels return to the square, tie a sliver of bark across the first hard word.

Let it rot in its time and be replaced by wood you did not force.

He tied the letter with a thin thread the bark-mender had given him—fibrous, strong, guaranteed to surrender when it should.

The caravan boy would carry it when he next went down for salt and stories.

***

On the fifth day, the bark-mender cut a thin ring from a storm-fallen branch—no thicker than a wedding bangle—and sanded it until it held sun like a small, obedient moon.

"For the cloth," she told Sid. "Hang it where the gold ladder shines."

They tied the ring to the cloth's lower corner with a knot a child could untie. When the wind moved, the ring tipped, caught light, and spilled it as a circle on the water, then on a cheek, then on a hand that was trying to be stubborn and forgot how.

"It remembers to move," the dervish said.

"It remembers to loosen," Sid answered.

***

By then, Sid knew: the valley no longer needed him the way Kherapur had once needed him.

It was making its own rules, hearing its own bowl, bridging its own bark. His work now was to do the hardest thing a weaver can do—to stop pulling when the row is true.

That evening, he sat with Viren, the dervish, and the caravan boy on the flat stone by the spring.

"We will soon go down," he said. "Before snow turns the cedar's lesson into a story you can only tell, not practice."

Viren nodded, looking pleased the way masters look when a student chooses the right time to leave the room he has just learned to love.

The caravan boy looked into the water, seeing there the track they had made and the track not yet made. "Will we go back to Kherapur first?"

"Yes," Sid said. "A loom that taught us to walk deserves to hear where our feet have been."

The dervish leaned back on his elbows. "And after?"

Sid smiled at the dark line where hills became sky. "We'll listen to thirst."

Bridge, don't strangle—leave space for mending that life itself will complete.

DSN

Chapter Twenty-Four – Snow on the Thread

The first snow came without warning.

One evening the cedar grove was only cold; the next morning, it was wearing white like a shawl stitched overnight by a sleepless sky.

The spring ran slower, the bowl's surface held the light in a quieter way, and the cloth on the frame seemed to grow heavier with every flake that settled upon it.

Sid rose before dawn to brush the snow from the loom. His fingers numbed at the touch of the wooden bars, but the gold ladder in the weave shone brighter than it had in the sun.

"It likes the cold," Viren said, joining him, steam lifting from his breath. "Gold always does, it remembers fire."

The young dervish stood nearby, hands tucked into his sleeves, eyes on the hills that were already disappearing into cloud. "The passes will close in two days," he warned. "If we mean to leave, we must leave now."

Sid nodded, though his feet were still rooted in the snow.

***

Word spread quickly: the weaver was leaving.

But the valley didn't come to crowd the square or bring farewell gifts. Instead, people worked their looms and mended their bark bridges as if nothing was ending.

It took Sid a moment to understand: they weren't ignoring his departure—they were practicing what he had taught them. The work had to go on whether the teacher stayed or not.

Only the bark-mender came to speak directly.

She placed a folded scrap of cloth in his hand. "It's from the first bark bridge I ever tied. It rotted this season. I wanted you to see what the tree made in its place."

Inside was a strip of new wood, pale and smooth, shaped by the cedar itself. Sid turned it over, feeling its lightness.

"You didn't make this," he said.

"I began it," she replied. "The rest was done without me."

***

That night, the three of them—Sid, Viren, and the dervish—sat by the cedar and watched the snow deepen. The pilgrim's bowl had begun to freeze at the edges, forming a lace of ice that curled inward like fingers.

"Snow is the thread the sky uses," the dervish said. "It covers every mistake until spring."

"Or it hides wounds so they don't fester in the open," Viren added.

Sid traced a fingertip along the frozen rim. "Maybe it's the pause before the next weave. No loom runs without rest."

***

On the second morning, the caravan boy returned from the lowlands, cheeks red, carrying a small leather pouch.

"This is from Kherapur," he said. Inside was a piece of dyed cotton—deep indigo, woven with a thin line of gold.

"They're still weaving ladders," Sid said softly.

"They said to tell you," the boy added, "that the well is full, and the arguments are not."

The snow in Sid's chest began to melt.

***

Before leaving, Sid and the others finished the cloth they had been working on since their arrival. The gold ladder ran its length, but now it was flanked by cedar-ring patterns and thin white stitches made from goat wool to mimic falling snow.

They left it on the loom, tied not too tight, just enough to wait for spring.

"If it's still here when we return, they will know we meant to come back," Sid said.

"And if it's gone?" asked the boy.

"Then someone needed it more."

***

On the morning of their departure, the valley sent no procession, no speeches.

Instead, as Sid walked past each home, a hand would emerge from a doorway to drop something into the pilgrim's bowl: a sliver of cedar, a thread of dyed cotton, a piece of bread wrapped in cloth, a tiny clay bead. By the time they reached the last cedar, the bowl was a map of the valley in miniature.

"Now we carry them," Viren said.

"Or they carry us," Sid replied.

***

At the highest pass before the descent, Sid turned for one last look.

The valley lay below like a woven cloth stretched on the frame of its hills—white threads of snow, gold glints where the sun hit the looms, and the dark green stitches of cedar groves.

He touched the pilgrim's bowl and the strip of cedar wood from the bark-mender, feeling how both were light enough to carry and heavy enough to matter.

The dervish spoke into the cold air: "What will we tell Kherapur?"

Sid smiled. "That peace is a thread you cannot store. It only holds if it's moving."

And with that, they stepped into the path that would lead them back to where the first knot had been tied.

Peace is not a thing to keep; it's a thread to keep moving.

DSN

Chapter Twenty-Five – The Return to Kherapur

The descent took three days, and with every turn the air grew softer, trading the bite of cedar wind for the lowland's damp warmth. By the time they reached the first fields of mustard—still bare, waiting for the rains—the snow on their boots had melted into the earth.

Kherapur announced itself the way it always did: not with its gate, but with the smell of its bread.

It was the same bakery where Sid had once stood in a queue long enough to consider leaving the city entirely.

Now, the line was short, and the baker's boy stood outside handing slices to anyone who passed.

"They began doing this after the ladders reached us," the boy explained, pressing warm bread into Sid's hand. "We thought it strange at first, giving away food without a festival. Now it's just … what we do."

***

The narrow lane that had once been a clutter of dye-vats and gossip now ran like a seam of gold.

From window to window, door to door, hung narrow cloths with the same ladder pattern—some crooked, some fine, some bright with saffron-dye, others muted with age.

It was not uniformity; it was recognition.

As they walked, people stepped aside to make way—not because Sid was anyone special, but because the pilgrim's bowl swung at his side.

It was full now, almost to spilling, each item inside a fingerprint of the journey: cedar wood, goat wool, clay beads, threads from valleys and villages that had once been names without faces.

***

When they reached the central courtyard, they found it already full.

Not a crowd clamouring for news, but a circle waiting in the way of a loom waiting for its weft.

The headman of Kherapur stepped forward, his gold-thread turban catching the light.

"We heard you would return," he said simply. "And we heard you might not."

Sid set the pilgrim's bowl in the centre of the courtyard and, without speaking, began to lay its contents out in a slow spiral: the cedar sliver, the indigo cotton from the caravan boy, a bead carved with a snowflake, a piece of bark polished smooth, the elder's knot of dyed yarn.

By the time he finished, the spiral reached the edge of the crowd.

"This is the map of where peace has been," he said at last. "If you want it to stay, you must keep it moving."

***

Instead of resuming his post at the market loom, Sid left it empty for a day, just as he had in the cedar valley.

Children climbed onto its bench, threading their own colours into small strips.

Merchants wove quick, rough cloths for wrapping parcels.

By evening, the frame held no single vision—only many small weaves knotted together.

"This is what peace looks like," Sid told Viren.

"Not perfect. Not mine. And not finished."

***

Before the first night closed in, Sid wove one final strip himself: a short length of gold ladder bordered with the cedar ring pattern. He hung it over the city's well, where everyone would see it and no one could claim it.

The dervish, standing beside him, asked, "Will you leave again?"

"Yes," Sid said. "And no. My hands may leave. My thread will stay."

***

That night, as they shared bread in the courtyard, a woman began to hum the same tune that had once accompanied the pilgrim's story in the cedar grove.

One by one, others joined—not in perfect unison, but in the way that threads agree without becoming the same colour.

The sound rose into the air and stayed there, hovering above the rooftops like a net catching the last light of day.

Sid closed his eyes. For the first time since he had left Kherapur, he felt that the bowl was no longer his to carry.

Peace is not the absence of struggle—it is the habit of carrying one another through it.

In a world where threads are spun not only from silk and cotton, but from memory, grief, and hope, there are stories that refuse to remain silent. They wait to be woven into the fabric of our days, until even silence wears their colour.

This is not a tale you have merely read; it is a breath that has entered your lungs, a rhythm that will walk with you long after the last page has closed. You will find yourself, in some forgotten hour, standing once more in the loom keeper's workshop—the air thick with the scent of raw yarn, the hum of the spindle echoing in your chest like a remembered prayer.

Every page was a shuttle, drawing you deeper into a tapestry where past and present entwine, where even the frayed edges are faithful to their purpose.

And now that you have walked the loom's length, carry this truth: the weave has entered your hands, your breath, your very being. You are no longer who you were. You are part of the cloth. And the cloth, forever, is part of you.

Epilogue

The Thread That Survives Fire

There will come a day when the shawl wears thin.
When the threads loosen.
When even the gold begins to fade.

And someone will ask,
"What did this ever really change?"

They will not have seen the first well,
the first stitch,
the first time someone spoke
without raising their voice.

They will not remember the boy
who walked beyond the dunes
with nothing but a cup
and a question.

They will not know
that once,
a village chose to weave instead of shout.

But someone, maybe a child,
will pull the cloth from a shelf.
Faded. Frayed. Forgotten.

They will trace its edge
and feel something stir—
not in the cloth, but in themselves.

They will not call it magic.
They will call it memory.
They will call it recognition.

That child will pick up a needle.
Not because they were told to,
but because
they remember
how the world feels
when it is being held
—not by law,
not by fear—
but by care.

And when they thread that needle,
even if the world is burning,
even if no one is watching,
even if they are the only one left who believes …

The weave will begin again.

The cloth will return.
Not as it was.
But as it is needed.

Acknowledgements

This book may have been written from my mind, but it was **held, protected, and carried** by the people who loved me even when I wasn't easy to love, or easy to understand.

It takes a village to raise a child, they say but it takes **an even nobler village to raise a wounded adult into a man capable of healing others.**

To **my village**, this book is your reflection.

To my parents

You taught me dignity not through sermons, but through the way you lived when no one was watching.

You held my uncertainties as if they were still my first steps, and you allowed my dreams to breathe even when they terrified you.

Everything I create in this lifetime is rooted in a lesson you taught without ever making it a lecture:

"The world may not always be kind,

but you must never stop being human."

If I have helped even one person heal, it is because I first learnt compassion from how gently you held me when I didn't deserve it.

To my wife, Aathira

My partner, my witness, and the quiet architect of my sanity.

Thank you for **loving the man I am**, not the mask the world admires.

Thank you for holding space for the days when I am a storm, for the nights I am unreachable, and the mornings when I am rebuilding myself from pieces that only you could see.

You have carried the emotional weight of my calling, my work, my absences, and my relentless pursuit of meaning, all while protecting our home, our child, and my unspoken fears. You gifted us not just family, but new bonds of the heart—a sister who became a daughter, and a brother our son found in Shreyansh.

You are not just a chapter in my life you are the paragraph I return to when every other page stops making sense.

To my brothers not by blood, but by battle—Jaideep & Sudeep

You entered my life at different stages of my life , but you stayed as **brothers forged through storms**.

We built dreams without guarantees, shortcuts, or safety nets. Just trust, sweat, sleepless nights, and the stubborn belief that we were born to do more than merely survive.

Thank you for standing beside me not only in achievements but also in the silent midnights where doubt sounds louder than faith.

If people see strength in me today, they are only seeing the confidence that grew because **you both refused to let me collapse alone.**

Finally…

To each of you. You did not just appear in my journey; you **carved me**, shaped me,

repaired me, and reminded me that love, loyalty, and presence are **the greatest forms of prayer.**

This book exists because **you all never gave up on the man who was still learning how to not give up on himself.**

Thank you not for what you did, but for **who you chose to be while loving me.**

About the Author

Dr. Sheetal Nair (DSN) is not merely a psychotherapist or author, he is a lifelong student of the human condition, a weaver of emotional truth, and a voice for the unseen, unheard, and unhealed parts of modern humanity.

Armed with multiple doctorates across psychology, human behaviour, and leadership, DSN chose not to sit behind credentials, titles, or academic pedestals but to walk directly into the inner wilderness of people, where theory collapses and raw truth begins.

Across boardrooms, coaching rooms, classrooms, and silent midnight conversations, he has held space for thousands from adolescents stitched with invisible expectations to corporate achievers trapped inside golden cages, from couples trying to remember love to individuals trying to survive themselves.

A 3-time TEDx Speaker, columnist, and mental well-being evangelist, DSN has built a growing movement around psychological safety, identity healing, and purpose-aligned living while staying deeply anchored in humility, family, and inner work.

Yet, if asked to name his greatest credential, he will not say his degrees, publications, awards, or stage history.

He will say, "My son."

For it was through fatherhood, not academia, that he learned his most life-changing truths:

That vulnerability is strength.

That love is a language, not a performance.

That healing is possible only when we stop fighting who we truly are.

Today, he continues his work from Vadodara, India, not as a guru, not as a hero, but as a peace enabler, weaving stories, systems, and safe spaces where people can finally meet the version of themselves they were always meant to become.

He does not aim to impress.

He aims to awaken.